Former naval intelligence officer and US Naval Academy graduate **Geri Krotow** draws inspiration from the global situations she's experienced. Geri loves to hear from her readers. You can email her via her website and blog, gerikrotow.com.

D1392351

THE PREGNANT COLTON WITNESS

GERI KROTOW

MILLS & BOON

First Published in Great Britain 2018
by Mills & Boon, an imprint of HarperCollins*Publishers*
1 London Bridge Street, London, SE1 9GF

The Pregnant Colton Witness © 2018 by Harlequin Books S.A.

Special thanks and acknowledgement are given to Geri Krotow for her contribution to *The Coltons of Red Ridge* series.

ISBN: 978-0-263-26599-6

1018

MIX
Paper from
responsible sources
FSC™ C007454
www.fsc.org

This book is produced from independently certified FSC™ paper to ensure responsible forest management.

For more information visit: www.harpercollins.co.uk/green

Printed and bound in Spain
by CPI, Barcelona

For Ellen—it's been a joy watching you turn into the beautiful young woman you are.

Acknowledgements

A special thank-you to Deanna Reiber, DVM, USA (Ret.) who provided me with veterinary insight and advice as only a USNA sister alumna can do.

Chapter 1

The Red Ridge, South Dakota, autumn morning sky streaked pink and violet across Black Hills Lake. Dr. Patience Colton, DVM, took a moment to soak it all in. Nestled in the northwestern part of the state, Red Ridge—and more specifically, the town's K9 clinic—were home to her. The only place her heart ever found peace. She committed the view of the mountains to memory, knowing there stood a good chance she'd never look at it, or anything, the same way again. It all depended upon the results of the simple test kit in the Red Ridge Drugstore bag that she clutched in her left hand.

No one had seen her yet; none of the staff knew she was already at the K9 clinic, ready for another day of veterinary medicine. She could run—but to where? Her townhome? Her cabin in the mountains? Another state, where her veterinary license wouldn't be valid? If the test proved positive, running wasn't going to change it or the overwhelming implications. Running away might be an option for another person, but not her. Patience never backed down from a challenge, and what might be her toughest yet was no exception.

She sucked in the crisp mountain air before she entered the building, hoping for a few minutes to herself to figure out if the signals from her body weren't random.

Fifteen minutes later, she wondered if maybe running away wasn't such a bad idea.

"No. Freaking. Way." Patience's hands shook as she spoke under her breath, staring at the test strip she'd used only minutes earlier to determine if she had skipped a period again for any reason other than stress. She stood in the restroom of the Red Ridge County K9 Clinic, *her* clinic, and struggled to get a grip. Locked in the staff bathroom, the weight of how her life was changing triggered a gush of tears. It had been a mistake to do this at work.

She couldn't be caught like this—crying over a pregnancy test result. "Calm down." She gave herself the same advice she wished she could give her K9 patients when they were stressed.

It hadn't been uncommon for her to miss one or two cycles while in veterinary school and also working extra hours at a part-time job to help pay for her expenses. And the last few months had been incredibly stressful, not just for her but for all of Red Ridge. The modestly sized town was in the midst of a criminal crisis. Patience worked closely with the Red Ridge Police De-

breasts. It hadn't been the smartest thing he'd done, giving in to his needs, but he had no regrets over their one-night stand almost three months ago. A surge of protectiveness toward that night—no, toward Patience—blindsided him. It wasn't fair to call it a one-night stand. It had been more. Or maybe he'd misinterpreted the obvious pleasure she'd enjoyed at his hands as more than the sexual release they'd shared.

He wasn't dating anyone regularly, how could he with four half siblings to take care of? But that night with Patience had reminded him that he needed some caretaking himself. And while both he and Patience had agreed that one night was all their lives allowed, both for time and family reasons, maybe they shouldn't have been so hasty in their agreement. He sure wouldn't mind seeing her again.

A beautiful woman like Patience was probably already involved with someone else. Although she'd said she wasn't, and that she had no plans to date anyone. She needed her personal life to remain simple, she'd said, because of the heavy demands being the K9 vet and community vet in general made on her. Didn't they all have demanding jobs, though, in Red Ridge? The small mining town was incredibly productive for its size, and required nearly every citizen to do their part to make the municipality thrive. Besides, if Patience was anything like him, no matter how busy life got there were those moments of realizing you were missing something... Yeah, maybe he'd ask her out again. Of course, that could lead to more than he was able to handle, but he wanted to handle Patience—

The house phone rang and he answered, cradling the receiver between his jaw and shoulder. "Maddox."

"Nash, it's dispatch." He recognized Shelly Langston's voice. She worked dispatch for Red Ridge County since he'd been on the force, and probably ten years before that. Shelly filled in whenever Frank Lanelli, the senior dispatcher, was off.

"What do you have, Shelly?"

"We've got a child who fell off a bike on the way to school, over the highway shoulder on Route 10. They want Greta on the scene."

"We're on our way."

He hung up and motioned for Greta, but she was one step ahead of him, at the door with her leash in her mouth.

"Good girl. We've got today's first job."

They worked as one, leaving the house, getting into the police K9 vehicle, arriving on scene and helping to determine if the child had fallen by accident or if a vehicle had forced them off the road. Greta used her expert sniffer to relay information and Nash translated to the officers and first responders. Immediately after they'd wrapped it up, they were called to a home burglary downtown, and then later, to the site of an arson. Before their shift finished, Nash and Greta had participated in no fewer than eight cases, from shoplifting to drug dealing to escorting a lost memory-care patient back to his care facility.

No matter how long the day grew, as tiring as the work was, thoughts of a brilliant evening with the lovely

Patience Colton never left him. Maybe he'd scrape up the nerve to call her. In an unofficial capacity, of course.

Patience looked at her staff, all gathered in the break room. Reception was closed after normal clinic hours, and they'd endured an especially long day of surgeries and urgent calls.

"That's it for today, folks. Unless we have another emergency call, I want everyone going home and getting a good meal and rest. This weekend could end up being just as taxing." She referred not just to the fact that the K9 unit was often busiest on weekends due to a surge in criminal activity, but the fact that weekends were when weddings happened. Most couples had quietly postponed their weddings once it was a clear a killer was targeting grooms, but everyone was on edge, worried that the Groom Killer could strike again at any moment. There were always couples who wouldn't let anything stop them from their big day.

"Do you think that the animals are trying to tell us something, Doc?" Pauline, the newest vet tech, didn't ask the question with cynicism. She was new and trying to absorb all she could about how the facility worked. The staff had discussed more than once the apparent connection between animal distress and human anxiety. Animals were empathic, and Red Ridge's pets had to be feeling the edginess of their owners these last months. It'd be abnormal to not be worried about the serial killer.

"It doesn't matter what I believe. It's fact that they seem to have an edge on us when it comes to predicting bad behavior, and to a T each patient has demonstrated the signs of stress brought on by a perceived threat. Our resident parrot has been squawking twice as much, the cats have been mewling no matter their pain level, and the dogs have whimpered at random times. While any of that could be coincidence, as we've had a high number of surgeries this week, I'm inclined to trust experience. Go home and get some rest—you could be called back within hours. Let's all pitch in and get Surgery cleaned up. I don't want anyone tackling that alone—we've made a mess!" Her staff laughed and she used the energy to buoy her through the next thirty minutes of a thorough scrubbing down of their operating room.

It was a mess from the day's routine spaying and neutering surgeries, and the unexpected gunshot wound. She'd spent two hours picking out birdshot pellets from a sweet labradoodle's right haunch. These were all in addition to the regular duties she had as the K9 veterinarian. The RRPD encouraged her clinic to help the community whenever possible. But her first duty was always K9.

Not to mention the personal connection. The Red Ridge K9 unit, training center and clinic were dedicated to the memory of Patience's mother, who'd died in childbirth. Her father, Fenwick Colton, lived up to his reputation as a wealthy, self-serving ass most of the time. But when it came to her mom's legacy and the K9 facility, Fenwick didn't waver. Until recently, when he'd threatened to shut down funding because of Colton Energy's dwindling bankroll.

Her father had put his family through its paces, fathering five children by three different wives. Her older half sister, Layla, was the only one from Fenwick's first marriage, while Patience and her older sister, Beatrix, were from his second trip down the aisle. After their mother died birthing Patience, Fenwick remarried again and had her younger half brother, Blake, and then half sister Gemma. While Patience enjoyed a pretty good relationship with all of her siblings, she'd always felt closest to Layla. She'd taken her cue from hardworking Layla, too, dedicating herself to veterinary work as diligently as Layla did to Colton Energy.

Which made Patience furious with her father for mismanaging his funds and putting the K9 program at risk. She was convinced that it was by no fault of Layla's that Colton Energy was struggling. If anything, Layla's contributions kept the company from going belly-up much sooner. Patience wanted to ask Layla more detailed questions about it but her caseload prevented her from digging too deep into the financial records. She trusted her corporate tycoon half sister to fill her in on the details. Not that Layla was thrilled to share anything with her. Not since Patience had blown up at her for agreeing to an engagement to that old geezer Hamlin Harrington. His son, Devlin, was Layla's age, for heaven's sake. But all Fenwick saw was that Hamlin's money would save Colton Energy and the Red Ridge K9 facility, and so that was what Layla focused on. As much as Patience loved her job, nothing was worth her sister's happiness. She'd begged Layla to call of the wedding.

Layla disagreed. Their epic fight had occurred hours before Patience had found blessed escape in Nash Maddox's arms.

Once the cleanup was done, she dismissed her remaining staff. Patience relished the alone time, a chance to pick through her thoughts over her family's conflicts.

She stopped at the sink and ran the hot water, hoping she'd still be able to convince Layla to come up with another way to make bank. While she was grateful that Layla's fiancé had postponed their wedding until the Groom Killer was caught, Patience still couldn't contain the revulsion she had toward her sister's fiancé. Naturally, their father wanted the killer behind bars so that the wedding could happen as soon as possible. Fenwick Colton was always about himself and his company and he'd stop at nothing to get the money out of Hamlin. Worse, Fenwick threatened to cut off his K9 endowment if the Groom Killer wasn't apprehended ASAP. Patience shuddered at what she'd heard her father tell the police chief. *Do your job or you won't have one.* Even as the mayor of Red Ridge, Fenwick was clueless as to the man-hours and emotional dedication required to nail down a hardened criminal, and it took that much more effort to corner someone as wily as the Groom Killer. But even her father's intimidation hadn't produced the killer, not yet.

"What are you going to do for dinner, Doc?" Ted Jones, the college student who volunteered as he waited to apply for vet school, spoke up as she washed her hands. Normally she didn't mind having a meal with him and answering his myriad questions on the application process, but she was spent.

"I've got a lot of food in the staff refrigerator, and it's

my turn to pull night duty. You go ahead and get out of here. Don't you have midterms to study for?"

"Yeah, I do. Thanks, Doc." He grinned and sauntered off. Patience enjoyed the camaraderie her staff shared, paid and volunteer alike. It was what had made her want to be the K9 vet for the RRPD. The sense of belonging and being part of a bigger picture had wrapped its arms around her the minute she'd walked in here three years ago.

Patience waited until everyone had left the building before she went back into her office and sat at her desk. She needed some time to ground herself before eating dinner and then starting the care rounds for the dogs and cats, and the one parrot they were boarding for an elderly woman who'd broken her hip and was in ortho rehabilitation for the next month. Patience opened her top desk drawer and gazed at the pregnancy test result from this morning.

"Well, look at that. Still pregnant." She giggled at her own joke, but her laughter turned to sobs as the enormity of her circumstances hit her. She was going to have a child and had no clue how to handle a baby. A puppy or kitten, sure, she could do that blindfolded. But a human child, her child?

Her father had been absent at best, throwing himself into his work and accumulation of wealth her entire life. Patience had never known anything but the selfish man Fenwick Colton was. Yet she'd never given up on him, or broken contact with her full and half siblings. Family was important to her.

A baby.

She was going to have a baby. Her profuse tears had to be from the hormones, since she usually prided herself on her self-control.

Loud guffaws sounded from the boarding area and she sniffed, unable to keep the grin from breaking through her tears. Mrs. Bellamy's scarlet macaw was hungry. Patience's stomach grumbled in response, and she wiped her cheeks with a tissue.

"Coming, Gabby!"

The brilliantly hued bird tilted her head in welcome and made kissing noises with her smooth white beak as Patience walked into the huge room and opened the birdcage door.

"How are you doing, sweetie?"

Gabby climbed out of her cage and onto the playpen atop her dwelling as Patience gathered some mixed veggies from the freezer and heated them in the microwave. The parrot let out a loud shriek that was half laugh, half scream.

"Stop it, silly. You still have plenty of pellets and nuts in your bowl, beautiful bird."

After Gabby was busy with her warm supper, Patience checked on her other charges. Most of the post-op animals were resting, the effects of anesthesia and their bodies' ordeals exhausting them. But Fred, the labradoodle gunshot victim, had his big brown eyes open and managed to wag his tail the tiniest bit when she approached.

"It's okay, Fred. You're doing great." The poor dog had done nothing to deserve the hit from a bird hunter's gun. It had been a legitimate mistake, as Fred had escaped his owner's yard via a broken fence post, and the hunter wasn't in a residential area. With his caramel coat, Fred had blended in perfectly with the South Dakota hills and underbrush. Fred and the hunter had been after the same duck. Fred had inadvertently saved the duck's life.

"What am I going to tell Nash, Fred? How will I tell him? He needs to know, so there's no sense trying to be all trauma drama and play 'I've got a secret' about this."

The dog's eyebrows moved as if he understood her dilemma. A part of her brain knew that Fred was a dog, and he was in the midst of serious recuperation, but as she looked around the room full of animals, he was her best bet.

She leaned in closer and opened the kennel door to stroke his sweet, fluffy head. "Let's pretend you're Nash and I go up to you. Should I go over to the RRPD? Or call him? No, can't do this over the phone. This is a serious matter. I'm having his puppy! I mean, his baby. My baby. Our child."

Gabby's shriek of laughter rent the room and Patience jumped. "Jeez Louise, Gabby, you scared me! But you're right." She gently closed Fred's crate door and went back to the macaw, who'd polished off her veggies and was scraping her beak clean on the cage bars. "Come here, sweet birdie."

Gabby promptly got on Patience's forearm and leaned close to her face. "Give me a kissy." Gabby's voice perfectly mimicked his elderly owner's and Patience laughed. As shocking and emotional as her day had started, this was the best therapy anywhere. Being with her animals. Of course, they belonged to their various owners, the K9s to their handlers at the RRPD, but while they were under her care, they were her responsibility. It was a sacred commitment.

Right now, Gabby needed some human touch and affection. And Patience needed to calm down before she faced Nash again, most likely in the morning, to tell him the news. They were having a baby. Well, she was. She in no way expected anything from him.

"Okay, Gabby girl, come here and I'll have you and Fred help me practice telling Nash."

The parrot stepped daintily onto the T-stick Patience used to handle the exotic bird to prevent a bite. She'd learned the method during her avian course in vet school. As much as Gabby wanted to be on her shoulder, Patience never allowed it. Just as she exuded an alpha energy around the K9s and other dogs, she kept birds from thinking she was a tree and her shoulder a branch by using the perching tool.

She walked with Gabby the few steps to Fred's kennel, which was at eye level.

"Now, you two tell me what sounds better. First choice—Nash, I'm pregnant and keeping your baby. I don't need you to do anything. You've done quite enough already." She looked from Fred to Gabby, surprised to find that they were both staring intently at her. Gabby was used to touring the dog kennel with other members of the staff for a break in the monotony of her cage. Fred wasn't reacting to the parrot as he had to the duck earlier. Of course, he was heavily sedated.

Since both animals didn't react, she tried again.

"Too serious? Well, having any man's baby is serious business, but I get your point. How about this... Hey,

Nash, how have you been since we hooked up after the K9 training session? In case you were wondering, your sperm is viable. I'm pregnant! Congratulations!"

Fred's tail gave a firmer thump than earlier and Gabby nuzzled her huge white beak into her brightly feathered chest, inviting touch. Patience gently scratched the back of the bird's nape, marveling at the silky soft skin under her feathers. Gabby made lovey-dovey noises, indicating her enjoyment of the contact.

"Okay, you both seem to like option two. I think it's going to need more work, though. I'll think about it and we'll practice again after dinner." She walked Gabby back to her cage and put her inside. The bird went obligingly but Patience had to coax one claw off the T-stick. "Sorry, hon. I know you'd rather be out, but your cage is the safest bet until I come back."

Back in the staff area, she heated up the leftovers from last night's dinner—or was it two nights ago?—and streamed two episodes of her favorite sitcom on her laptop as she ate. She had to make a concerted effort to eat as nutritiously as possible, especially now.

She was going to be a mother. Have her own family. Thinking of it, the prospect was at once terrifying and thrilling. She had shared a bumpy relationship with her father since she'd gone to college and vet school on her own, scraping and saving to pay back every cent of her loans. Fenwick had watched in exasperation, trying to convince her that she didn't have to make things so hard on herself. She had her own trust fund.

But Patience had to know that her degree and career

were hers. It wasn't another freebie from being born into a rich family.

Her phone lit up with a call from Layla. Patience considered ignoring it; she wasn't about to tell anyone she was pregnant until she told Nash. And even then she wanted to keep this to herself for a bit. As the phone vibrated, she put it on speaker.

"Hi, Layla. What's up?"

"Where are you? I need a drink. I want you to meet me downtown." Layla sounded just like their father. Her harsh countenance grated at times, same as Fenwick's. But unlike him, she was soft and kind underneath her hard corporate exterior.

"I'm on duty." Thank goodness. Patience wasn't ready to face her half sister yet. Layla always seemed to sense what was going on with her, as different as they were. "I'm tied to the clinic all night." Not completely true, as she could call on a volunteer to watch the patients at any time. She was still miffed at Layla for getting engaged to Hamlin Harrington. No business, even Colton Energy, was worth a marriage of convenience. Screw the millions Hamlin promised Fenwick he'd pour into the utilities company.

"We had a labradoodle come in with birdshot and I need to make sure he stays comfortable through the night."

"Oh, that's awful! Who would do such a cruel thing?" More proof that Layla had a kind heart. She loved animals as much as Patience did.

"It was an accident, truly. Trust me, if I thought it was foul play I'd have called the RRPD." Animal welfare was a safe topic with Layla, who was otherwise too preoccupied with her corporate role as Colton Energy VP for Patience's liking.

"Make sure you report it if you change your mind." Layla never seemed to realize that Patience had her DVM and was fully capable of deciding when and why on the calls into the RRPD. Not to mention her K9 certification.

"What are you up to now, Layla?" She heard the hard edge in her voice but it couldn't be helped. It rarely could with Layla.

"Since my sister can't meet me for a drink at the only decent bar in town, I think I'll spend more time here in the office. There's always more to do, and I'll need to have things in order for when we have our cash flow back in the black."

Patience gritted her teeth. Layla was goading her. When it came to the subject of Layla's secret engagement with the smarmy Hamlin, silence was the best approach.

"Patience?"

"I'm here." She rolled her eyes and popped a grape into her mouth. Good thing they were on speakerphone and not doing their usual video call.

"You know your judgment is stinking over the line, don't you?" Layla's tone was pure corporate executive with a dollop of big sister.

"I haven't said a thing!" Either the grape had been sour or she was reacting to Layla's tone, for her stomach began to roil. She'd felt fine for the most part, until she realized she was pregnant. And thought back to how shaky her stomach had been the last couple months. Another reason to put off meeting Layla. Her sister would connect the dots in an instant if Patience turned her nose up at food and, of course, alcohol. Gourmet meals paired with fine wine were the one luxury Patience indulged in, and only with Layla, on occasion.

"You don't have to say anything, dear sister. I do think Hamlin cares about me, by the way. Dad's putting pressure on us to make it legal ASAP, but with the Groom Killer around, Hamlin's rightfully nervous. I know you don't approve of us or how we're handling our engagement. But it is what it is, little sis. I'm doing what you always say you believe in and putting family first."

"By keeping it secret?" Stung by Layla's accurate assessment, she couldn't help but to strike back.

"From the public. There's a serial killer on the loose, or have you forgotten?"

Patience remembered she was alone in the K9 clinic, and saw the darkening October sky through her office window. The early sunset was a sign of the winter to come, not a harbinger of more killings. Her body thought otherwise as shivers ran down her spine.

"Of course I haven't forgotten. But Hamlin's just like our father. His priority is always business and that means Colton Energy. Above all else, Layla, even your marriage." She almost choked on the word *marriage*, and yet guilt tugged at her. How could she judge anyone, even Hamlin, for postponing the nuptials? A psycho intent on killing grooms remained at large. Even if Hamlin had the resources to provide himself with the best security on the planet. And she had to admit, if only to herself, that she was a hypocrite. She'd been relieved that the wedding was called off for now. The thought of Layla on Hamlin's arm made her sick, and it had nothing to do with baby hormones.

"Tell that to Bo Gage, Michael Hayden, Jack Parkowski, Joey McBurn or Thad Randall." Layla's sharp reply sounded as if she was a woman sure of her place in life, but Patience saw through her sister's smoke screen. Red Ridge wasn't a tiny town, but it was small enough that they'd both known all five victims, at least as acquaintances. "And the RRPD still hasn't caught our cousin Demi—if she's the killer, of course."

Layla referred to Demi Colton, a bounty hunter whose relation to the murders was circumstantial at best. Patience didn't know Demi well as they hadn't spent a lot of time together growing up, or now as adults. But she didn't believe the gossip one bit, not since Demi brought in an injured dog to the clinic shortly before she'd fled. Demi *cared*. Killers didn't.

"She's not. She's only a suspect."

Demi had left town right after Bo Gage, the first victim, had been found. Because Demi and Bo Gage had been engaged for a week, until he'd dumped her for Haley Patton, there was circumstantial evidence, as well as motive, for Demi's guilt. It made no sense to Patience, though, because Demi had zero relationship to the other victims. But community opinion named Demi as the killer. Fortunately, the RRPD worked with facts, as did Patience.

Patience had to stand up for the truth, even if they flew in direct opposition to popular opinion. She put her trust in the RRPD's investigative capabilities over fear-fueled town scuttlebutt.

Layla's silence grew long and Patience wondered for the umpteenth time if her sister needed her to talk her out of the Hamlin Harrington agreement.

"Layla, you know I admire your loyalty to Colton Energy and our father, even though he doesn't deserve it. And we haven't talked about it since the fund-raiser, for obvious reasons, but are you sure you still want to marry Hamlin?"

"Of course I do." Her prompt reply was too quick, too reactionary. "Look, I'm not the one who went off the Colton straight and narrow. I'm holding up my part of the family business." Nice dig at Patience, who'd eschewed accepting the family legacy of becoming a financial wizard, like her father and sister. Finances had never appealed to her; serving others had.

"That doesn't mean you have to marry a man you don't love."

"Who says I don't love him?" Didn't Layla hear the lack of conviction in her own reply?

"Please. We can agree to disagree about your engagement, but we need to drop the pretense that you care for Hamlin if we're going to remain sisters." Patience would never have been so direct even a day ago. Was the baby giving her some kind of relationship superpower? Where she was realizing the preciousness of life and wanted to protect her bond with her sister?

"I wish I could tell you more, Patience, but you're going to have to trust me. I know what I'm doing."

"I'm here if you need me, Layla. Let's meet sometime next week, after I get through this weekend."

Layla's sigh sounded over the phone's speaker, and Patience felt sorry for her sister—almost. It was her decision to become involved with Hamlin, a man their father's age and just as disagreeable and greedy when it came to business. They weren't wealthy by accident. Although Fenwick's recent investment blunders were bleeding the company funds to near bankruptcy. From a pure economic standpoint, Colton Energy was desperate for what Hamlin Harrington offered.

Gabby's screech reached through the walls. Layla gasped. "What was *that*?"

"Our resident parrot. She's ready to come out of her cage again and stretch her wings. I'll give you a call later tomorrow, when I'm off duty, okay?"

"Maybe we can meet for a meal, then? With a nice bottle of red. My treat." Layla's infectious optimism made Patience laugh. It'd be soda water for her from here on out, but Layla didn't need to know that yet.

"We'll see."

Chapter 2

Patience managed to get all the animals taken care of by eleven o'clock that night. Her legs thanked her as she lay down and stretched out on the folding bed assigned specifically to the overnight watch. She rotated the duty with another local veterinarian, who worked for the clinic on a contract basis, and the vet assistants. She'd thought that finding out she wasn't just bloated or had gained a few pounds, but was in fact pregnant, would keep her up all night. What did she know about being a mother? And what was she going to say to Nash? How was she going to tell him? How could she make sure he completely understood that she wanted nothing from him, needed nothing?

Snuggling into the rose-printed down comforter she'd brought from home, she promised herself she'd worry about it later. She had a few hours before the next rounds. She fell into a sound slumber that lasted until the alarm on her watch pinged at 2:00 a.m.

She blinked in the stillness, her mind blank for a brief second until reality seeped back in. Her entire life had changed only hours earlier with the positive sign on the pregnancy test's pee stick. Stretching her arms and legs, she chuckled in the inky dark. Who was she kidding? Her life had changed almost three months ago after the K9 training seminar with Nash. They'd made this baby while the summer sun was still shining, before autumn was more than a thought. And now the fall was passing quickly, the cold arctic winds beginning to dip down into the mountains.

Anxiety mounted at the task ahead of her and she sat up. Her job at the moment remained to care for her animals—the clinic's caseload.

Patience mentally ran through the patients that needed to be checked and, in particular, walked. Fred was the only canine needing a walk, unless some of the other dogs asked to go. Moving through the familiar steps she'd done countless times when she'd had night duty gave her comfort in the midst of the chaotic change a baby added to her life. But it didn't erase her exhaustion. No wonder she'd been dragging the last month or so. It wasn't the change of season or heavy workload— she was pregnant!

As an extra bribe to herself to get up and get going, she planned to take a look at the trees surrounding Black Hills Lake in hopes of spotting a great horned owl. There was a family of the majestic birds that roosted in the nearby fir trees, but the nocturnal animals were difficult to spot most nights and impossible in daylight hours. Tonight, with the full moon and predicted clear skies, she hoped to see one of the creatures' unique silhouettes.

Patience loved the squeaks her sneakered feet made on the floors when the clinic was closed and she had it all to herself. It was just her, the animals she loved so much and the sense of purpose being a K9 veterinarian gave her.

The motion-detector lights came on as she walked through the corridor that ran along the back of the building. No sounds came out of the kennel. A good sign. This time of night it was usually silent, but if an animal were really ill, this could be the worst time for them, too. She let out a breath of gratitude as she saw that all the animals were quiet and resting peacefully in their respective kennels. The usually feisty Gabby had her head tucked firmly under a wing, one eye peering at Patience as if to say "Don't bug me."

"Hi, sweetie girl," she whispered to the parrot as she walked by.

Fred was her main concern. The labradoodle needed to get an easy walk in, not so much to relieve himself as to help with the healing and to prevent his muscles from freezing up. He acknowledged her with half-open eyes, a tiny wag of his fluffy, untrimmed tail. She smiled at his sweet face. "Come on, boy. Let's go for a little stroll."

She braced her core muscles as she gently half lifted the eighty-pound dog onto a portable ramp and onto the clinic floor. How had she not noticed the way her stomach was beginning to bulge out? She'd had strong abs all through vet school, as it was essential to being able to do her job well. And while the strength was still there, she was going to have to start modifying her routine soon. Heat crawled up her neck. Had her coworkers noticed her changing shape and simply remained quiet out of pure professionalism?

No, her sister would have noticed if she looked heavier or larger in her belly area. Layla was all about keeping up appearances. If it wasn't such an ungodly hour Patience might be tempted to call Layla and share her situation. But then their father would find out, since Layla worked so closely with him and it'd be almost impossible for her to keep her mouth shut. Patience loved her sister and they shared a close bond, but it was probably best to keep this news to herself for the time being. She'd tell all her siblings—Layla, Bea, Blake and Gemma—when she was ready. She ignored the obvious: Nash Maddox needed to be told first.

Snapping a collar and leash onto Fred, she waited for him to steady his legs before they walked to the exit. "Here you go." She wrapped a dog jacket made from space blanket material around him, being careful not to touch his suture area. Normally a large dog like Fred wouldn't need a coat, but right after surgery it was her clinic's protocol, and the night temperatures were dropping precipitously as autumn faded and winter hustled in. She'd had what—three, four winters in her clinic so far?

Her clinic. She'd worked so hard through vet school,

hoping to work with K9s, never dreaming she'd land such a plum job. It was a plus to be able to live and work near her family, even when they demonstrated a multitude of reasons she might want to consider a job elsewhere.

And now she was expanding the Colton family by one.

Yes, the everyday physicality of her job was going to need some modification as her pregnancy progressed. Lifting heavy dogs was going to have to take a back seat to her baby's safety. That was what the other staff members and volunteers were for. She'd get through it.

She shoved gloves on and zipped up her ski jacket, bracing for the cold mountain air. South Dakota in October was not only desolate but could be bone-chilling. Thank goodness it hadn't stormed today, and there was bare, dry ground for Fred to relieve himself on. Having to take care of his needs on sticky mud or frozen snow would have been tough on her patient.

"Here we go, buddy. Get ready for some cold." She draped the binoculars they kept on a hook near the door around her neck. Still no sign of clouds, so she might see a great horned owl, after all. Ever since she'd been a little girl she'd loved searching trees for birds. Identifying them played second fiddle to enjoying their unselfconscious way of living. And who didn't want to watch a feathered creature fly?

The air didn't disappoint—it was freezing—as she and Fred stepped into the fenced yard area where the dogs could run free, whether they were boarders or healing from treatment. It was atop a hill, on the way to the mountains, and overlooked Black Hills Lake. The yard sloped down to where the RRPD had installed a small concrete pier for training purposes. The insides of Patience's nose stung from the harsh temperature, but the beauty of the view was worth it.

"How are you doing, Fred?"

Fred didn't respond to her verbal inquiry, but sniffed the ground and in short order lifted his leg against a small bush. A burst of relief filled her, warming her from the inside out. Nothing was more satisfying than to see a patient recover quickly and return to normal. As Fred resumed sniffing the frosty ground, she looked up at the stars that speckled the dark sky, the full moon their only competition. She and her canine companion could stay out a few minutes more before the cold became a concern for Fred's healing body.

A creaking sound floated through the air and she turned her attention to the lake. It was beginning to freeze over with a thin crust of sparkling ice, but was too deep to solidify in just one cold night. A movement caught her eye and she noticed a small boat in the middle of the lake, approximately two hundred yards from shore, dead center from where she and Fred stood. Patience blinked, hoping she was imagining the warning signals from her tightening gut. It was too early for ice fishing and too late, as well as too cold, for anything else recreational.

Something very wrong was happening on Black Hills Lake.

She raised the binoculars with shaky hands and focused on the boat. What she saw seemed out of a nightmare. A tall figure, masculine in stature, was holding the limp body of a woman in his arms, her slim limbs hanging lifeless. At least Patience believed it to be a woman, as the figure had long hair. The pale gold strands hung over the man's arms and reflected the moonlight. Her gut tightened painfully and Patience held her breath, waiting for the woman to wake up. *Wake up!*

Before she could yell to let them know they were being watched and should cease whatever they were doing, the man dropped the woman over the side of the boat. There was no struggle, nothing but the soft splash as the body disappeared from sight. As if it'd never been there.

Patience couldn't stop the gasping cry that escaped her lips. Her exclamation, while not at top volume, carried across the eerie stillness. Frozen in place, she kept the binoculars focused, noting whatever details she could.

Icy shock crept over her as the man turned toward the clinic, searching for the source of the sound. She saw the moment he spotted her on the shore, his ice-blue eyes clear and sinister in the moonlight, through the binocular lenses. She didn't recognize him, but knew that he saw her, and his frown was the only warning she had before he leaned over and started a high-power motor she hadn't noticed before. Patience dropped the binoculars to her chest and scooped up Fred, adrenaline lending her strength. She'd lifted heavier dogs before, but she never had to move this quickly with them.

"Hang in there with me, Fred." She ran back into the clinic and quickly put him in his kennel. Her phone was on her desk where she'd left it, but she had to lock the back door before running for it. When she turned the standard lock, she looked through the window and noted that the boat had carved through the thin layer of lake ice and the hulking man was close to the shore behind the clinic. He was clearly aiming for the small pier that the RRPD used for its launches and when training the K9 divers.

Patience went into alert mode, following the protocol practiced in drills with the RRPD. She locked herself in her office, grabbed her phone and went to the gun safe as she called the dispatcher.

"Nine-one-one. What's your emergency?" Frank Lanelli's familiar, confident voice eased her nerves as she rattled off her circumstances. All the while she unlocked her gun safe, took possession of her weapon, ensured it was loaded and then climbed under her desk, her designated safe spot.

A shot rang out and she couldn't keep from flinching. She knew the killer must have gotten through the outside security fence by now, which she told Frank.

"The shot I heard had to be him breaking through the outer gate."

"Good action, Patience. You locked the back door up tight. That will slow him down, too." Frank had known her since she was a kid and had five children of his own, whom she'd gone to school with. He was an anchor for the Red Ridge County emergency dispatch system. "Where are you now?"

"I'm in my office—the room closest to the kennel, farthest from the clinic's back entrance. I'm under my desk with my .45." She heard a crash and instinctively tightened her hold on her weapon. "I think he just broke a window." She couldn't help gasping for breath.

"Where are you, you bitch?" The man's roar reverberated through the walls.

"Oh, no. He's coming for me, Frank." Frantic, she tried to focus, figure out what to do next.

"Hang on, Patience. Was that the intruder yelling?"

She clung to Frank's voice. "Yes. That was him. He's angry and calling me a b-b-bitch." She could barely breathe as fear's noose tightened the muscles around her chest, where her heart raced. She felt its beats on her thighs, pressed up against her as she was folded under the desk. And against her baby bump. Her *baby*. Please, please let her make it through this. For the baby if nothing else.

"You're good, Patience. You locked your office door?"

"Yes."

"And turned off the lights?"

"Yes, but he has a weapon—"

"Tell me what you hear, Patience." Frank's voice remained steady and clear.

"He's calling for me. He's going to kill me, Frank." And the baby. The baby no one but she knew about.

"No one's going to hurt you, Patience. You're doing great. You have your weapon ready to go. Keep me on the line. Keep talking if you can. If you have to put your phone down, keep it on, okay? Two units are en route. You're certain you saw a body go into the lake?"

"Yes, positive." She repeated the details of what she'd seen. "Even if she was alive, there's little chance she still is. She looked unconscious, or dead, and the water is too cold."

"Okay, we're dispatching one K9 team now. That will be Sergeant Maddox with Greta. They'll go straight to the lake. You stay put until the other RRPD units arrive."

All she heard was Nash's name. Nash would make it okay. He was an accomplished, practiced, proficient K9 officer.

Frank continued with the running commentary, but even his professional expertise, his years of calming traumatized citizens, couldn't soothe her. There was an intruder in her clinic, most likely a murderer. The doom that shrouded Red Ridge over the Groom Killer had nothing on the dread that choked her. Had she found out she was going to have a baby today only to lose everything at the hands of some evil stranger?

A loud crash, followed by the sound of splintering glass hitting the clinic's floor, sharpened her senses. He was breaking the kennel windows that lined the corridor. The dogs started barking and Gabby shrieked in outrage. *Please don't let him hurt the patients.*

"Where are you? Come out now or I'll take out your precious animals!" And he had a weapon to make good on his promise.

He was closer, too close. Patience tightly hugged her knees, weapon ready in her right hand. She'd do whatever she had to do to stay alive and protect her baby.

"One minute out, Frank." Nash spoke to dispatch, his siren blaring as he raced through town in his RRPD K9

SUV, Greta secured on the back seat. His entire shift had been routine until Patience's call came in from the clinic. He had to help her, to reach her before the suspect did. He kicked himself for not calling her, asking her out again. And then immediately shoved that thought aside. There'd be time for self-reflection later, after Patience and the clinic were secure.

"Go ahead to the lake, Nash. We've got two units approaching the clinic."

"How far out?"

"Three and four minutes." Frank's concern was audible. "Repeat, K9 officer is to go to the lake. Victim in the water."

"I hear you. But I'm going into the clinic first if no other unit is there yet." Nash was only a minute out, and seconds could mean the difference between life and death. He'd be damned if he let anyone harm Patience. He strained to see up the road, willing the clinic to appear.

"You're right, Nash—we need you to go to the clinic first. We've now got a crazy man in the kennels, threatening Dr. Colton. She's armed."

"Copy that. Clinic first." Like it was going to be anything else. A victim in the cold depths of the lake, even with his and Greta's expert abilities, stood a slim chance of making it, if any. There was still hope for Patience.

Damn it. Why hadn't he called her, reached out to her after their night together? If he got them through this, he'd make it up to her.

Greta whined in the back seat.

"It's okay, gal. We're going to get there." Greta never

made a sound unless reacting to her instinct that something was wrong. That made two of them. It was constant these days in Red Ridge, from the Groom Killer case to the incessant pace of drug crime.

The clinic buildings came into sight, and as they appeared on the horizon Nash expelled a harsh breath. He willed the vehicle to go faster, faster as he navigated the familiar road. The security lights were blazing, but no inside lights were visible. He also noted no sign of RRPD units, confirming Frank's reported ETA for them, so Nash pulled around to the back, next to the fenced area for the dogs and K9 training.

Wasting no time, he got Greta out of the vehicle. With his weapon drawn, they ran for the building. Greta needed no orders, for they'd practiced and served together thousands of times. They were more than K9 partners; they were a team.

Nash went to let himself in through the secured fence, ready to punch in the code known only to himself as the lead K9 officer and Patience. His gut sank when he saw the broken gate, proof of forced entry. Together he and Greta ran to the clinic's rear entrance, where he found shattered glass on the concrete doorstep, the door ajar. He signaled for Greta to jump over the sharp shards.

"Come on, Greta!" Employing the moves that were second nature to them, Nash and Greta went through a coordinated series of tactics that allowed him to ensure the way was clear, while she remained on alert for any unusual sounds or scents. Several of the windows that looked out onto the lake and lined the corridor had been smashed, but Nash noted that none of the animals in the kennels appeared to have been injured, and only a few were yipping or meowing in distress. The loudest of the bunch was Gabby, the bird Patience boarded so often she was becoming a familiar sight. What wasn't usual was the huge red parrot's screams that threatened to split his eardrums.

"Help, help!"

The parrot's cries were downright spooky as he and Greta moved forward through the dark corridor. *Patience*. He had to get to Patience.

Chapter 3

Patience grasped her .45 and aimed it at the office door. The thug continued to pound on it after firing once, and it was beginning to splinter around the handle. She stayed steady behind her desk, resting her arms atop it, ready to shoot. Mentally, she recalled all she'd learned at the firing range, and in various training scenarios the RRPD had put her through in the rare event she'd ever need to protect herself or the K9s. She'd never expected someone to break into the clinic to come after her, though. To steal the valuable K9 dogs, sure, or to score prescription painkillers for street sales—specific crimes the clinic was at risk for. But to have a murderer break in and come after her? Not expected.

Adrenaline surged as she prepared to shoot, but she

maintained her steady focus on the door, visualizing the shape of the man she'd take down.

And then…nothing. Footsteps running away. Sharp barks, more footsteps.

"Patience, Nash Maddox is on scene with Greta." Her phone, on speaker, barked into the quiet office.

"You mean at the lake." Despite the silence she remained ready to shoot. Her mind heard Frank's calm explanation, but her nerves weren't ready to stand down.

"No, he's come to ensure your safety and apprehend the assailant." Sirens reached her ears. "Stay put as he clears the front reception area."

"Okay." She heard Nash's deep voice echo through the halls, heard Greta's bark as the K9 team secured the clinic.

"RRPD is on-site, Patience." Frank's relief was evident. "Nash and Greta chased off the suspect, turned over security to the other RRPD units and are headed to your office now."

"Thanks, Frank." She let out a shaky breath, but still couldn't let go of her weapon. What if the man had circled around back?

A knock sounded on the damaged door, followed by a deep bark—Greta's.

"Patience, are you there? It's Nash." Greta's second bark let her know the huge Newfoundland wanted to declare she was there, too.

Slowly, Patience unfolded from behind the desk. "Nash is at the door, Frank."

"Affirmative. You can let him in, Patience. Repeat, he's chased off the intruder and our units are on-site."

"Patience?" Nash's voice reflected concern, even muffled by the door.

"I'm here." She unlocked the door and opened it, and was immediately engulfed by Nash in a bear hug. His arms pressed her to him, his solid, hard body the most comfortable thing she'd ever felt. Patience melted against him and let herself receive his warmth.

"Thank God you're okay." He placed his free hand, the one not holding his Glock, on her shoulder, and his eyes blazed with intent as he looked at her. "Are you? Okay?"

"I am. It was…" In a totally uncharacteristic move, tears fell from her burning eyes and she fought to speak. "I'm sorry. This isn't like me."

"It's just the shock. I've had to fight tears on ops before, too." He wiped one cheek with his thumb, then the other. She relished the rough, calloused slide of his skin against hers. It grounded her, allowed her to stop gulping for air.

"Thanks, Nash. You're right. It's shock, I guess."

"And some adrenaline." He dropped his arm and looked her over. "Did you hit anything while you were diving under the desk?"

"No, really, I'm fine." She rubbed both eyes with the heel of her hand, and realized that she, too, still gripped her weapon. "Except I didn't know I was still holding this." She engaged the safety and placed it on her desk. "I think I used everything I ever learned in our practice drills over the last twenty minutes."

"You probably did. And you handled it perfectly, from what I can see." As she looked into his eyes she saw his conviction, and it chased away the dark cloud of anxiety that the killer had left in his wake.

"Where is he now?" Quakes of relief started to move through her. She'd done it. Nash had helped. The killer was gone.

"Hopefully, in custody. He took off toward the mountains. The RRPD will get him." Nash sounded certain, but she wasn't so sure.

"A man who's so cold-blooded as to…to dump a body in the lake like that?" She shook her head. "He's not going to get caught. Not this easily. I'll bet he has a getaway car stashed nearby."

Nash put his hand on her shoulder again. "That's not your problem anymore. You're safe. The clinic is secure. Get some water or coffee." He nodded at the teakettle behind her desk.

"Okay." Her stomach heaved at the thought of ingesting anything, but tea might be good. *Her stomach*—had Nash noticed her midsection was thicker?

"Stay put until the other officers show up. They're here now, I think. Greta and I have to run to the lake."

His attention was focused on the case at hand, not her burgeoning baby bump. She had to tell him. But not now, in the middle of a crisis.

She tried to offer him a wobbly smile. "The man came up in his boat—it's on the shore at the bottom of the clinic property. You could take that out to where I saw him dump the body." Shivers raced up and down her spine. "Nash, be careful. He's—he's going to kill you if he can."

"He's not going to hurt anyone else, Patience. You're

safe now." He repeated that, as if he understood just how shook up the entire circumstance made her. "I'll be back for you." He paused, and for a moment that hung between them like eternity she thought he was going to kiss her. His eyes glittered with promise, one not solely related to the dark happenings of tonight. Dare she read anything into his heated stare? But instead of placing his lips on hers, he offered a wink instead. "Be right back."

Nash and Greta disappeared into the corridor, and as she watched through the broken windows, they raced out the door and across the training area toward the lake, their movements in perfect unison. Her instincts told her to go into the kennel and calm her patients, but Nash was right—she needed to wait until she knew the entire property was safe again, that the killer hadn't come back.

"Dr. Colton!" Officer Maria Ruiz caught her attention, waving from the other end of the corridor. Relief swamped Patience. If Maria was here, then what Nash said was true. The building was secure. For now. She'd feel better when he was behind bars, when the mental image of him sneaking back to kill her didn't seem an inevitable outcome to her hyped-up brain.

"Maria. Thanks for clearing the place."

"It's my job." Maria looked at her, then peered out a window toward the lake. The K9 team was in the boat after the evidence team quickly dusted it for prints and searched for evidence. The launch made its way toward where Patience had seen the woman's body being dropped. "That Officer Maddox and Greta in the launch?"

"Yes. They're headed for the center of the lake, by the dive platform." Patience had a hard time reconciling the spot with where they trained the diving K9s and sometimes sunbathed during the summer. "It's where the suspect was when I saw him with the woman."

Maria nodded. "Yeah—the other K9 unit is already there. See the other launch? They just said Greta's going to be diving." She looked around Patience's office, checking every cranny and under the desk before she was satisfied. "You should be safe in here for now. How did the man get into the clinic to begin with?"

"I heard a gunshot when he was still outside. I think he must have broken through the security gate and then smashed a window to unlock the back door."

As she replied Patience realized how slim the chances were that the thug was able to not only expertly break through the eight-foot security fence, but also enter the clinic so quickly. "He had to be trained to do this. Or knew the codes." But then that would mean someone they trusted was a criminal. Or maybe one of her staff had unwittingly given information to the wrong person.

Maria watched her with a gravity reserved for their toughest cases, reflecting Patience's concerns. "That he knew the codes seems unlikely—we'll check to see if he actually shot the outer gate, and determine exactly how he got in. At the very least he has a good understanding of the clinic's layout, judging by how quickly this escalated. The fact that he came right to your door…"

She assessed Patience with a compassionate gaze. "Do you want to come out back with me?"

"Sure." There was nothing she'd like more than to see the assailant caught, or better, the woman he'd dumped into the lake still alive and okay. And staying in her office alone right now wasn't high on her list of fun things. Patience needed to be with people, and Maria's grounding presence fitted the bill.

They walked past the kennel and Patience noted that most of the patients were amazingly calm, even with the wide-paned windows shattered. "We'll be back, everyone."

"Do you think they understand they're okay now?" Maria spoke as they reached the back door, which had clearly been broken through, its window also smashed.

"Absolutely. Gabby, the parrot, is being quiet—that's telling. When she gets riled up, she can incite a puppy and kitty riot in there, let me tell you."

Maria laughed. "At least your sense of humor hasn't left the building. That's a good sign."

"Probably." She wasn't feeling particularly jovial, but more like punch-drunk. The adrenaline comedown affected everyone differently. The baby's welfare gnawed at her. Adrenaline flooding her system was bad enough; it couldn't be great for the baby. She had to make an appointment with her doctor soon, and get a referral to an ob-gyn if necessary.

Thoughts of the baby's needs took a back seat as they approached the open gate. Patience saw bullet holes in the area surrounding the keypad.

"I've got to take photos and gather evidence." Maria pulled out a plastic evidence bag.

"Of course. I'm going to see if I can watch the dive ops from the deck." Patience jerked her thumb over her shoulder, indicating the clinic's small pier. There were a half-dozen launches used for K9 and police diving exercises and ops. Three were out in the center of the lake. "Thank you, Maria. I wouldn't have left my office if you hadn't shown up."

"No problem."

Once she was on the deck, looking across the icy water, it hit Patience how close the killer had come to reaching her. The fact she'd made it back to the clinic and managed to lock the door was incredible, seeing how easily he'd broken through the fence. It had felt as if she'd run miles with the recuperating labradoodle in her arms, but it had been less than a hundred yards. Too close.

Her heartbeat raced and she closed her eyes. The baby needed her to be calm. Patience reminded herself what Nash had emphasized: she was safe. But the woman the man had dumped in the water—probably not. Patience quickly refocused on the dive operation.

With the binoculars still around her neck, she used them to watch the divers from the shore, ignoring the cold as she shivered in her jacket. It was clear that Greta wasn't having the luck she was expected to, as Nash and the other K9 officers repeatedly encouraged her to go back under, to find what they knew was there. The woman with the long pale hair. Finally, Greta's large head surfaced and Nash's arm signaled for the other officers to help. Patience made out something in Greta's mouth as several shouts from the assembled RRPD officers echoed across the water.

"We have something!"

"Positive contact!"

"Pull her up!"

The rescuers got the body on board a slightly larger RRPD vessel normally used in the warmer months when boaters and swimmers got into trouble. EMTs who'd joined the op worked over the woman, valiantly attempting to ascertain if she'd survived, or had a chance of life once at the hospital and warmed back up. But the pit in Patience's stomach confirmed what she already knew—there was no way the victim had survived her chilling plunge.

"Good dog." Nash gave the hand command for Greta to shake herself off, and she did so, her huge bulk moving with unexpected grace aboard the small launch. The woman Greta had found was unresponsive and already being transported to the Red Ridge Medical Center, on the off chance she could be miraculously brought back to life. Nash wasn't expecting good news, though, as she'd been in the water for too long. There was a gash on her forehead that appeared lethal. He suspected she'd been dead already when the killer dumped her.

Frustration that the killer had gone free chased away the relief he felt over Patience's survival. Someone cold-blooded enough to kill and dump a woman in the chilly lake waters wouldn't have hesitated to kill a possible witness. Thank God Nash and Greta had made it there in time.

"You're a good girl, Greta." He petted her, wet fur and all.

"They both are good dogs." Officer Mike Georges stood next to him, his Belgian Malinois, Rocky, under a space blanket. Mike had been first on the scene and Rocky had dived for the woman with no luck. It was common knowledge that Greta was their best water dog, but Rocky was well trained, too, as were the several Belgian Malinois on the K9 team. Still, Nash couldn't help the surge of pride at Greta's job well-done.

"I'm sorry I didn't get out here sooner." Nash knew that it didn't matter—they'd all been too late to save the woman. Still, he'd had an option and he'd chosen to rescue Patience from the intruder over heading for the lake. He'd do it again, even if dispatch hadn't agreed.

"We both know it wouldn't have made a difference, unfortunately. And we were here at least five minutes ahead of you, with no luck." Mike's face was grim, softening only when he looked at his K9. "Is Dr. Colton okay?"

"Yeah. She was armed for bear and ready to take out the jerk."

Mike nodded. "She was a great study when we did our training last time. And her shot is perfect—as good as any officer's."

"I know." And he did. Nash knew a lot about Patience Colton that would cause Mike to raise his bushy eyebrows. More than he should, in fact, for a woman he'd known only one night, no matter how incredible.

He couldn't help noticing her whenever she was in the vicinity, or listening extra carefully when one of the other police officers mentioned her name in passing.

"I'm going back to check on her. She can give Greta a quick look over, too." He knew Greta was okay; the dog was bred for cold water activity. Newfoundlands excelled at pulling half-ton nets full of fish, as well as soaked men, aboard ships in the northern Atlantic. A quick dip into the bone-chilling lake in the middle of autumn was all in a day's work for Greta. In fact, judging from the dog's smile as she panted, she wouldn't hesitate to jump back into the water. It was in her DNA.

Still, Patience insisted on looking over all the K9s after they'd performed any particularly demanding task, or had worked for an extended length of time. Another reason she was so respected by the RRPD. Dr. Patience Colton cared for her charges.

"You look like you need a rest, too, Nash."

"I'm good." He'd be better once he was with Patience again, saw that she was doing all right. She'd set off his internal warning radar as quick as any one of the kids. More so, in some respects.

"Okay, then, I'll see you in there in a bit. Rocky's going to do a sniff check around the clinic and then we'll go see if we can figure out what direction our man in question headed. I'll take Rocky into the clinic for his check after that."

"Juliette and Sasha will be in on that, won't they?" RRPD Officer Juliette Walsh was dating Patience's brother, Blake, and was the K9 partner to their strongest sniffer, a beagle named Sasha.

"For sure, but we can help, too." Mike nodded at the streaks in the eastern sky that heralded sunrise. "We may as well finish out the morning. See you back at the station." They'd reached shore and Nash was relieved to see at least six patrol cars, lights blazing, parked alongside the clinic. He knew Patience was safe, but he still felt the tight band around his chest loosen as he drew closer. As if he was the one person who could keep her safe.

It was purely his concern for a colleague. And okay, he felt a sense of responsibility because they'd had that night together. Which underscored why he wasn't in a place to get involved with anyone. If he was this connected to Patience after only one night of sex, along with working together, he'd be doomed if he seriously dated anyone.

Patience isn't just anyone.

He shrugged off his annoying conscience and nodded at the RRPD officer guarding the clinic entrance, who let him pass.

Greta followed alongside him, down the long corridor to Patience's office. But they didn't have to go that far; he saw her in the kennel, through the portion of the glass wall that was still intact. She was talking to another officer, but when she saw Nash her expression softened and she gave him a half smile. Before he could acknowledge her silent greeting, however, the smile faded and creases appeared on her forehead. He remembered them in a different context, when she'd broken apart in his arms, her orgasm shaking both of them. But she wasn't in his arms now, and this expression wasn't that of a woman in the throes of passion. Patience looked worried. As if something about him made her anxious.

Patience stopped Maria midsentence.

"I'm sorry, but will you please excuse me? I've got to examine Greta."

She walked up to Nash and Greta, waiting in the main corridor.

"Nash, wait."

He turned around and she couldn't read his expression.

"I—I should take a look at Greta. Please bring her into the exam room."

She didn't wait for him to answer, but shoved open the door to the large space. Within seconds she'd lowered the stainless steel table in the middle, and Nash led Greta to stand on it. He held her by the harness while Patience grasped the dog's collar, then used the foot pedal to raise the examination table. Nash removed Greta's harness and stepped back to allow Patience the space to care for the dog.

"She's fine. Just wet," he stated.

Nash's bond with Greta gave Patience the first sense of normalcy since she'd seen the woman's lifeless body slip into the lake. She mentally shook the image away.

"How long was Greta in the water?"

"Not more than twenty minutes tops. She dived four, five times before she found the victim."

"It was a woman." Patience wasn't asking. She knew what she'd seen.

"Yes. And she was deceased. They tried to revive her, but…" He grew quiet. Hypothermia and longevity in cold water weren't something he had to explain.

"But they couldn't. To be honest, I thought she was dead as he held her. Nothing I can prove, of course, but that's what my gut told me."

"Gut instinct is there for a reason." Their gazes met and it was as if Nash tried to communicate something else. Did he regret they'd only had one night together, too? Patience broke the eye contact and turned back to her examination.

"You did good work, Greta." She spoke softly to the canine, pausing to shoot him a quick glance. "Has she shown any signs of distress?"

Patience felt along Greta's abdomen, her flank. As she pressed her stethoscope to the dog's rib cage, she was acutely aware of Nash being so near.

"No, she's good. Another day of work for a Newfie, right, Greta?" He spoke with ease to his K9 partner, underscoring the tangible bond between them.

"She's fine. Good to go. We can get her dried off in the grooming area." Patience lowered the table and Greta promptly walked over to Nash, then plopped down. "And she'll need to rest for the remainder of the day. It's normal for her to be a little more tired—that water is frigid."

"Yeah, I was worried when she had to dive down more than a few times. I'll keep her harness off until she's completely dry." At the concern etched in his face, Patience realized with a start why she'd been attracted to him in the first place. The reason she'd given in to her desire and agreed to their night of passion. His dedication to duty, his ability to put others before himself. This was a man raising his four half siblings. How many men in their twenties would do that? Warm, tingling awareness lit up her insides.

"What?" He looked at her as if he'd heard her thoughts.

The result of her attraction and their shared night was so obvious to her as she stood in front of him, her belly on full view under her scrubs. While she knew no one else might notice yet, it would be a matter of days or maybe a week or two before her weight gain became obvious. Heat spread over her chest, up her neck. *Now or never.*

"Nash, we need to talk." Could she sound any more commanding? This was not something to break to him in a rough way. "Can I make you a cup of tea, coffee? There's hot chocolate in the break room, too, if you'd prefer."

His face went blank before his steely determination returned. "Uh, no, thanks. Yes, we do need to talk. Not here, though. I have to escort you to the police station so that you can file a report."

Her heart sank at how professional he sounded. And for good reason. The sooner she gave her report, the more accurate it would be. The better chance of providing a tidbit of information that might aid in apprehending the suspect. She needed to tell Nash she was having his baby, but it would have to wait. Again.

"I anticipated that. My standby is on duty now, for the duration. I'm free to give a statement." And go home after and sleep in her bed, which sounded divine. "As soon as we get Greta dried off, we can go."

Nash nodded, and she sensed a tension in his body. It could be the adrenaline from such a demanding op. But when he looked up at her, she saw vulnerability.

"Patience, I'm so sorry. I've been an ass. I should have contacted you before work put us together again. I've thought about you often since our night together." His eyes shone with what could be longing, attraction. Nonsense—he was tired from the recovery op.

"No worries, Nash. Why don't you take Greta to the grooming station and use the power driers? The sooner she's dry, the sooner we'll all get to bed."

Her face immediately heated. If Nash noticed her self-consciousness over the unintended reminder of their night together, he didn't reveal it. He had Greta by her leash and his hand on the door. "I just wanted to say that I'm really glad I got here when I did. Tonight."

Of course, that was what he was going to say. Patience swallowed, knowing in that instant that telling him he was tied to her forever as her baby daddy was something she had to do pronto. But not here, not in the midst of trying to find a murderer.

"Thanks. Me, too. If you hadn't shown up when you did, I know I'd have had to fire my weapon." She couldn't stop the shudder that ran through her. And she wasn't the shaky type. Digging deep, she tried to find the woman she'd been just yesterday. The uncompromising K9 veterinarian who knew what she wanted. Instead of the emotional wreck she felt like, wondering how on earth she was going to raise a baby.

Nash's hand dropped from the door handle and he closed the few feet between them. His touch was firm, warm, reassuring as he squeezed her shoulder. It was meant as a collegial reassurance, so why did it send lightning bolts of awareness through her?

"You didn't have to use your firearm. And if you had, you'd have protected yourself. You're a brilliant veterinarian, Patience, but you're also a great shot. I was there on the firing range with you during our last weapons refresher, remember?"

She nodded. "I do. Thanks, Nash."

He flashed his trademark sexy smile at her before he led Greta out of the room. Patience listened to their footsteps, walking in sync as they always did. Nash and Greta made a great team.

And now they were going to have a baby to fit into their routine. *If* Nash wanted to participate as a father. She'd thought for certain he wouldn't, but the man who'd protected her tonight wasn't the kind who balked at a challenge. And helping to raise a baby while still the guardian for his four half siblings would be the challenge of a lifetime.

Of course, he didn't know about it yet. She wished she still had the clinic all to herself, because she needed to talk to labradoodle Fred and scarlet macaw Gabby most desperately now.

She needed the words to tell Nash Maddox she was pregnant with his child. Yet the image of the woman going into the water, the terror that had sliced through Patience when she'd thought the killer would harm her and the baby, put a dreadful pall over such happy news. Now she understood how the would-be brides and grooms all over Red Ridge felt. The threat of being murdered trumped the desire to host even the most joyous occasion.

Patience squared her shoulders. No one would harm her child or erase the thrill of anticipation at his or her existence. But even as she made the silent vow to herself, a shiver of knowing rushed over her.

The Lake Killer wanted her dead.

Chapter 4

Nash ached from being out in the cold on that boat for so long and directing Greta during the recovery dive, so he knew her bones had to still feel the chill, no matter how thick her coat. He turned the doggy blow-dryer on High and maneuvered the corrugated plastic tubing in a methodical motion over her fur.

"You've got a lot of hair here, girl." She stood in patient compliance as he worked his fingers through her long black curls, taking care to lift all the way to her undercoat and get her thoroughly dry. He swore Greta loved it when he had to act as her hairdresser.

He chuckled. "It's okay, Greta. You've earned this tonight."

He wished he could have put Patience more at ease. She was the cool and collected veterinarian he knew as she'd examined Greta, with no remnants of the panicked woman he'd held an hour earlier. Except for the lines at the edges of her mouth; they let him know she was still wrung out over the night's events.

And she'd said they needed to talk. Had she been thinking about their time together, too?

Greta let out a happy croon and he laughed. "Are you reading my mind, girl?"

"Great work out there tonight, Nash." Maria walked into the grooming room.

"Thanks."

"I thought I'd let you know that we're wrapping things up in the clinic. It's secure for now, but we can't guarantee the suspect won't come back." She spoke loudly enough for him to hear over the drier.

"Yeah, I'm going to bring Dr. Colton to the station with me to give her report. As soon as this beast is dry."

"Patience agreed to that? To you driving her in?" Maria's brow rose. They all knew how independent Patience was. She ran the clinic single-handedly and never missed a beat. This was the first time she'd been threatened by the crime that had come to Red Ridge, though.

He nodded and shot his colleague a grin. "Yeah, she did, for now."

"She handled it better than I might have." Maria was a rookie but a tough one.

"Don't sell yourself short, Maria. All you're lacking is time in service. You're as well trained as any of us, and a better shot." And she knew it. Nash knew what was going on here—he'd mentored countless rookies as they entered RRPD service. It was a tough life but rewarding. A calling.

"Thanks, Officer Maddox." She ruffled the dog's damp fur. "And you, too, Greta."

"I've got it here. Thanks for finding us."

"How long is it going to take you to dry her?" Maria's glance took in Greta's bulky form, her huge paws, her long black, shaggy coat.

"Until she's dry." He rubbed Greta's chest as he focused the drier there. "Seriously, though? Another half hour or so."

"Better you than me." Maria's eyes followed the fluffs of black hair that floated through the air.

"No way you'd consider joining K9?"

"I love dogs and all, but what you and the other handlers have is a connection with your partner that I don't see myself having. Unless the right dog comes along, I'm a better fit for street patrol."

"That's fair. See you back at the station, Maria. Good job tonight."

"See you."

He wanted Greta dried yesterday. It was time to get Patience to the station and her report filed. And he'd have to approach the thought that had formed in his head.

Patience had no business being alone without police protection until the assailant was caught.

The RRPD station was bright inside, voices loud, drawers slamming as Nash and Patience walked to his desk. It was as if it were noon on a weekday instead of nearly five in the morning after a long night of unexpected operations. The aroma of fresh roasted coffee hit his nose, and while his stomach balked at the thought of it at this hour, his brain needed the clarity. He stopped by the coffeepot and looked at Patience. "Coffee?"

She blanched. "Um, no. Water is fine."

"Sometimes a case can take my appetite away, too." He poured himself a large, steaming cup, then reached into the small fridge for a bottle of water and handed it to Patience. Away from the clinic, she appeared a bit out of sorts.

"Thanks." Her fingers wrapped around the bottle, and his brain, the sex-starved part of him, flashed back to their night together, and all the delicious things she'd done with her hands on him. And her mouth. He had to stifle a groan.

"Hey, Nash!" Juliette Walsh slapped him on the back, crashing through his distraction. "Did you hear? Sasha got a good track on the suspect." Her pride in her beagle partner beamed from her face.

"Hey, Juliette. No, I hadn't—that's great. Any idea where he is now?"

She shook her head and looked at Patience, then back to Nash. "No, it seems he had a getaway car. It was gone by the time we tracked it."

"That sucks, but I'm glad you got that far." His gut sank at the revelation. He'd hoped they would luck out and catch the loser by now. If he was as much of a professional criminal as it looked, he might never get caught. Nash turned back to Patience. "Let's find a place to get your statement."

"Lead the way." She waved at Juliette. "Give Pandora a hug from me." Pandora was Juliette and Blake Colton's three-year-old daughter. Nash wondered if Patience was close to her business-investor brother, Juliette's boyfriend. He knew so little about Patience's personal life. It was best, of course, to keep things uncomplicated. Although if he were to get to know a woman more than as a one-night stand, Patience was the woman he'd pick.

Nash greeted each officer they passed as he and Patience headed for the conference room. It took a bit of time, as everyone wanted to greet their favorite veterinarian and also say hello to Greta, who thrived on the attention. Patience looked more weary with each step and he was anxious to get her seated.

He opened the door to the conference room, only to find it crammed with officers debriefing the case.

"Of course it's full," he said.

The anxious look stamped on her beautiful features tugged at him, deep in his chest. She'd been quiet in the SUV on the way here, and her obvious distress at being nearly attacked by a murderer had kept him from trying to draw her out. "We can go back to my desk."

She bit her lip as she glanced into the conference room. "I was hoping we could be alone for a bit. I have to talk to you, Nash."

"Do you mean you want to speak to the police counselor? It'd be totally natural after the night you've been through." He listened to his siblings' issues day in and day out, but he was far from a professional.

"No, I'm fine with all that. Tired, a little shaken up,

but that's not what I want to discuss with you." Impatience edged her tone.

Great. She was going to put the kibosh on any chance they'd repeat their one night of escape from their staid Red Ridge lives. Well, he didn't have to end his fantasy about being with her again. Not yet.

"We'll talk later. Right now, let's get your statement. Then I'm going home with you."

"Okay. Wait—what?"

He noticed there were flecks of amber in the dark brown depths of her widened eyes. Eyes that had glowed with pleasure that one night.

"You can drive me back to the clinic after we're done here," she said. "Please. I'll take my personal vehicle home."

He shook his head. "Not a great idea, Patience. The killer's on the loose and he visually ID'd you, remember?"

"It's not something I'm ever going to forget." White teeth tugged on her full bottom lip again, making Nash hard, not something proper in uniform. He couldn't look away from her sensuous mouth if he wanted to, and his awareness of her reached a supernatural degree. In the midst of a huge murder investigation, in the wee hours of the morning, in a boisterous police station, he wanted her.

"Let's get your statement."

As he turned, he almost ran into Red Ridge Police Chief Finn Colton, Patience's cousin.

"Nash—and Patience. Glad you're both here. You did great work on the lake, Nash. Greta." Finn nodded at the dog before focusing entirely on Patience. "How are you doing, Patience?"

"I'm fine, Finn." Her pale skin and tired stance didn't match her reply.

The chief remained silent, studying her. Nash wondered if she was going to break down again. To his surprise and unexpected relief she smiled and stood up straighter. "I made it through due to the training you and the department have always made sure to include me in. I can't thank you enough, Finn."

"Glad to hear it. You're giving Nash your statement?" To his credit, Finn kept it brief and businesslike. Exactly what Nash knew Patience needed in this moment. Heck, he needed it, too, about now. The less emotional any of them were, the quicker they'd get the work done and capture the murderer.

"Yes, right now." Patience's grit impressed him.

"Well, I'll let you two get to it. Nash, I need a quick word with you."

"Yes, sir." He looked at Patience. "Go ahead and wait for me at my desk."

"No problem."

Nash walked to Chief Colton's office, but his mind remained on the woman he left alone. Patience did that to him, made him unable to focus on anything, anyone but her. It should concern him, as his job required his full attention. But it didn't. Patience, and the feelings she stoked in him, felt damned good.

When Nash came back to his desk Patience saw the strain in his face.

"What did Finn want?"

"We lost the victim. As you suspected, she was dead before she hit the water."

"Do we know how he did it?"

"Yes. He gave her a lethal injection of fentanyl."

She didn't have a reply as she stared at his chiseled features and berated herself for noticing the shadow of his beard, wondering how the scruff would feel against the skin of her thighs. Either the pregnancy hormones were kicking her libido into overdrive or sex was a way to escape the gravity of their situation.

Or you have feelings for Nash. Nope. She wasn't going there.

He sat in his chair and they worked on getting her report filed.

Patience saw the tightness in Nash's jaw as she gave him her description of the suspect. She knew she was the reason he clenched his teeth. The sexual tension between them should seem ridiculous in the midst of their work. He'd just told her the woman at the lake had been murdered before Patience saw her body being dumped. And yet the sexual awareness only intensified the longer she and Nash were together. She wondered if he was afraid she was going to try to get him to meet up with her again.

If she weren't pregnant, facing such a life-changing event, she'd do it. She'd meet him again and let him work her body into a frenzy with those magic hands of his. Hands whose fingers now flew over a laptop keyboard as he entered the pertinent details of what she'd witnessed, up until he and Greta had shown up.

"You said you thought his hair was blond?"

"Or gray—it was hard to tell in the moonlight. Don't forget his eyes. They were a very particular shade of icy blue." She had the shivers again. Nash's fingers paused, his gorgeous eyes focused on her.

"Take my jacket—over there, on the back of the door."

"Thanks." She stood and retrieved the navy blue RRPD cold-weather jacket from the hook, not caring that it swamped her. It was warm, cozy and—damn it—smelled of Nash. As if being in the same room with him wasn't enough to remind her of how completely open she'd been to him that night, the night they'd conceived the baby. Her child. *Their* child.

No, *her* baby. She was going to raise him or her on her own. It would only prove disappointing later if she started to think Nash would want to be a fully invested father. He'd already had four kids to care for before he was thirty years old.

"What exactly did he say to you in the clinic?"

Nash's question brought her back, and she spent the next hour going over every painstaking detail of the night. Finally, Nash pushed back from his desk. "You look exhausted, Patience. Let's go to your place and get you settled for some rest." She noted he was careful not to mention getting her into bed. Smart man.

"I'm perfectly capable of driving myself home, Nash. I'll need a ride back to the clinic to get my car."

"Sorry, no can do. Greta and I are taking you home and, well…" He scratched the back of his head and his sandy hair reflected the overhead light.

"What are you saying, Nash?"

"I'm going to stay with you."

"That is absolutely not necessary. I have a weapon." She'd locked it back in its safe in her office, but she could get it and take it home.

"On you? All the time?" She damned his inscrutable professional bearing.

"Well, no, but I'm not usually worried about running into a murderer. Look, I'll pick up my weapon when you take me back to the clinic to get my car. And don't you have four brothers and sisters to take care of?"

"Four, ages twelve to seventeen. And they're fine. Our neighbor Mrs. Schaefer stayed with them last night. I phone her whenever I have a middle-of-the-night call." His emotional investment in his family impressed her. "They can be on their own as needed, since the oldest, Paige, can watch the younger ones. It's her schedule as a high school senior that is the deal breaker. She's off to marching band practice by six, three mornings a week. And while the rest can get themselves dressed and fed, it can get a little chaotic with all those teenagers under one roof."

Patience couldn't help but laugh. "I can't imagine. I know I think I'm busy at the vet clinic when we get a spike in patients, but I have a team helping me. And they're animals, not teens with the ability to get away with whatever they pretty much want."

"They're all good kids. I'm lucky. So far." He stood. "What I was starting to tell you is that I'd originally planned to take you to my place until we catch the killer. It'd be easier, for sure. But we have to assume you're being followed by the suspect until we know you're not. We can't lead the murderer to a house full of innocent kids. It's best for me to stay with you. Before you argue, the chief has ordered it. Think of it as not me being your bodyguard—you know cops don't do that. I'm hanging with you in the hopes of catching the bad guy."

"I love being mouse bait."

"You're not bait as far as the RRPD is concerned. You know that, though." He looked frustrated. "We have to keep you safe, Patience. Greta and I get the job."

She thought of trying to get him to change his mind, but Finn had ordered it. And truth be told, if she needed protection, there was no one else she trusted more. She'd heard the thug calling for her, knew his intent. Her life was on the line. What Nash didn't know yet was that along with her life, so was the baby's. She could use the backup, at least for the next few hours while she tried to get some rest.

But how was she supposed to sleep with the sexy Nash Maddox in the vicinity?

"I'm so sorry for the inconvenience to you and your family, Nash. Your brothers and sisters must hate your job at times."

"Like I said, it's all taken care of on my part. I have an aunt and uncle on their way into town, to help out for as long as I need. Aunt Clara was my mother's sister, and she asks to see the kids whenever it's convenient. She and Uncle Jim live in Sioux Falls and regularly make the trip. They'll stay for the duration of the case."

"What do you mean by 'duration'?"

"As long as it takes to ensure you're no longer a target."

He stood in front of her, but left a respectable distance between them. She was grateful because the combination of the long night, being with him in such close proximity for the better part of the last hour, and his overwhelming masculinity were making her feel as though she'd do whatever he asked her to. He wanted to move into her house? No problem. She could have the guest room ready in minutes. Or even better—her room. *Shoot.* She needed room to breathe before she did something stupid in her hyped-up-by-pregnancy hormonal state.

Your attraction to Nash has nothing to do with the baby.

"Nash, I appreciate the concern, but really, I'm okay. I'll sleep better knowing I'm not a burden to anyone." As he kept looking at her, the heat of desire unfurled low in her belly and she glanced away. "I suppose you're right. Just for the rest of today, though. After that I'll manage on my own."

"We'll worry about tomorrow later. And as for being a burden? You've got that wrong. It's my job, Patience."

Nash's dedication to duty, one of many things that attracted her to him, suddenly took on a different facet, as she was painfully aware of wanting to be more than just another case. Maybe it was finding out she was pregnant with his child, or the resulting hormones, but whatever it was, Patience couldn't deny it.

She wanted to be more than a case detail to Nash.

"I'm surprised you don't have any pets of your own." Nash sat on her sofa, where she'd laid out sheets, a blan-

ket and pillow. He'd forgone the guest room, as it was
too far removed from the rest of her house. He needed
to be right near the front door and kitchen entrance, both
within twenty feet of one another. Patience hadn't ar-
gued, which clued him in as to how exhausted she was.

She sipped at a spicy-smelling tea she'd made for
herself, and assessed him from the kitchen island. Her
open-concept house made it welcoming and easy to
converse, but he wasn't thrilled with the lack of walls.
Fewer obstructions for the murderer to break through,
less resistance to a bullet.

"I get my fill of animals at the clinic. I'd love to have
my own dog and a few cats, but for now, this is easier.
I spend the majority of my time at work these days, so
it's like having my own pets."

"Yeah, it's been a busy year for Red Ridge." He was
too tired to mentally review all the criminal activity,
but there had been plenty. Record breaking, in fact.
The Groom Killer was still out there, and now the Lake
Killer.

"You sure you'll be comfortable out here? I promise,
the guest room bed is practically brand-new. Only one
of my sisters slept there."

"Layla, Gemma or Bea?"

"Layla." She didn't elaborate. In a place like Red
Ridge, with Fenwick Colton as the energy mogul, everyone knew the entire Colton clan. Nash had had to
revisit his prejudices against the wealthy family when
he'd first started working with Patience. She was the
exact opposite of having a sense of entitlement.

"Answer me one thing, Patience."

"Okay."

"Why did a rich girl like you want to be a veterinarian? Have you always like animals?"

"I'm going to ignore your 'rich' comment. Why should my family's financial history have anything to do with my vocation? Or with me choosing what I want to do?"

"Jeez, I'm sorry. I was honestly curious. It seems to me you could have become whatever you wanted to. I'm impressed that you went through vet school and were hired to run the K9 clinic."

The wall she'd erected over her expression fell, revealing the Patience he'd made love to for several hours just a little under three months ago. She made her way to the sofa, where she sat on the end opposite him. He tried like heck to not mentally revisit that night, at least not while she was so close.

"I've never been interested in finances or being an entrepreneur. Science and math were my mainstays through school. My counselors suggested med school, dental school, even joining the military to become a physician. But I knew how much I loved horses and dogs, and it was natural for me to pick vet school."

"Your parents supported it?"

"I'm sure my mother would have. She's been gone a long while, as I'm sure you know. My father, he's a tough bastard. I love him unconditionally, but he's always made it clear what matters to him."

"Money."

"Right. The bottom line. That's just not who I am."

Nash watched, incredulously, as tears filled her eyes,

making their normally brown hue a rich, dark amber. They matched the highlights in her hair. Holy hell in a handbasket, what was he doing, noticing her hair color? He was reacting like his twelve-year-old brother. Jeez.

"Patience—"

She held up her hand. "I know a lot of people probably think I got the clinic position because of my father's endowment in my mother's name. But I competed fairly against applicants from all over the country, and even some overseas. I won my job fair and square."

"Of course you did. It's obvious in how well you do it. I'm sorry, Patience, I didn't mean to come across so tough."

The air between them shifted and he felt the intimacy of that special night return, at about the same time he noticed trepidation in her eyes.

"Nash, I have to tell you something." He'd heard that tone before—when a woman meant business. Usually the breaking-up kind, not that he'd had anyone to break up with these last several years.

"Save it, Patience. I know what you're going to say. And I get it. Please don't mistake my professional concern for personal interest. Don't worry, I'm not going to ask you to go out again. We made a deal that night—and I understand you don't want to break it."

Her eyes not only filled with tears, but he saw one, two, *three* spill over her long dark lashes and track down her creamy cheek. "Aw, Patience, I didn't mean for that to come out so rough."

"You don't get it, Nash. This isn't about us getting together again, but it is about that night."

He felt a kind of tingly awareness in his gut that had nothing to do with his attraction to her. His inner prescient warning system, the talent that helped him as he and Greta sought out evidence or conducted rescues, was going full-bore. What was she trying to tell him?

"What is, Patience?"

"I didn't want to tell you like this." She wiped at her cheeks.

"Tell me what, like how?" Was she going through an adrenaline comedown? He felt low after a hard call, but never wept.

"Like this—at eight o'clock in the morning after we've been up all night, after I saw a murder, or at least the last part of it, and Greta had to dive to find the body—"

"Spit it out, Patience." He heard the growl in his voice and it was like when frigid lake water hit his face. He stood up and paced away from the sofa, giving them both needed space.

Greta remained unruffled, lying on her side and only thumping her tail when Nash walked by. She'd also had a long night.

"I'm trying to." Patience wiped at her eyes with the sleeves of the fuzzy sweater she'd donned over her pajamas the minute they'd arrived.

"I hate this, Patience. It's as if you're afraid of telling me because of my reaction. As long as we've worked together, have you ever known me to overreact to anything?"

Clear brown eyes met his. "I'm pregnant, Nash. The baby's yours. I mean, you fathered the baby. But it's my baby. I'm going to raise it on my own. I completely understand that you have four siblings to raise and your kid calendar is booked for the next half-dozen years. But you should know it's your baby, and again, you're free to not worry about it."

Nash heard nothing more after Patience said, "I'm pregnant." Of course, he knew in his gut it was his kid. Unless Patience was more social than she'd let on, she'd been on her own and single for quite some time. If he could trust her, he'd been her first in a long while, and he doubted she'd been with anyone since. Not just because he hadn't, but because he knew how busy the K9 unit had been, which spelled extra hours for the clinic.

Looking around her great room, he decided her sparse furnishings and stacks of magazines and unopened mail on the kitchen counter validated her assertions and his assumptions. She was a loner in every sense of the word, except for their foray into unbridled passion three months ago.

"I believe you. I know it's my baby." Only then did it hit him, really register. He was about to become father to a child.

Chapter 5

Patience wanted to grab the words and shove them back down her throat the second she'd said them, right before Nash's features froze and his eyes glazed over. Relief soothed her upset stomach, though, indicating she'd done the right thing. Of course, she had—she and Nash were adults, and they'd both made the decisions that led to now. To a baby.

"This was a terrible time to tell you. I'm so sorry." She wasn't sure if he felt the constant pressure she had since she'd witnessed the murder, if he felt like someone was continually watching them.

"There's never a great time to drop news, is there? How long have you known?" He stood there, hands on hips, clearly processing.

"Since this morning. I mean, yesterday." Had it been

only twenty-four hours ago? "I thought I'd skipped my period from stress, like I used to during college and vet school. I should have known better. I'm a vet, for heaven's sake. But I never thought to do a pregnancy test until the last few days. The stomach bug I thought I couldn't get rid of, the exhaustion, the bloating—it's been the baby all along."

"I'm not blaming you for not telling me sooner." He sounded sincere, looked...calm. Too calm.

"I didn't know sooner! Look, I told you, you don't have to worry about me coming after you for support of any kind—financial or otherwise. You know I'm able to support this child with my job." She refused to mention her trust fund—that wasn't on the table. Patience prided herself on being able to fully support her life, and now the life of her future child. Without any of her family money, other than her reserve for an extreme emergency, or to maybe pay for her child's college.

"Of course, you can support a child." He looked sty-mied, speaking in the most general terms. "This isn't about finances, though, is it? We both have good jobs. And security, more than if we were running our own businesses."

"And I'm planning to work right up until the baby comes, take some maternity leave, then go right back to working at the clinic." She realized that while she hadn't consciously thought it all out, some part of her had been sifting through her options since yesterday morning.

"You're keeping the baby? For sure?" He looked at Greta as he spoke. The dog had perked up, her ears alert. As if she expected them to have a fight about it.

"Yes. Yes, I am. Have you heard anything I've said?" Hadn't he listened? Anger flooded her as she watched him, finding his attention was clearly not on her words. He was totally focused on Greta now, and the dog was issuing a long, low growl.

A loud rattling at her door, followed by a gunshot, was Patience's only warning before she was thrown by Nash onto the carpeted floor beside the sofa, then covered by Greta's body. The dog lay alongside her, shoving her up against the couch and placing herself between her and any bullet. Patience shoved her head under the upholstery skirt, the one place she could breathe freely without Greta's coat in her face.

She heard Nash shout, heard him fire his weapon, then a return shot and the sound of glass hitting the tiled foyer. *Not again.*

Nash had fired at an intruder.

"Stay down!" He gave the order to Patience. Greta knew to keep Patience covered until he released her; they trained for this all the time.

He caught a glimpse of a tall male figure with a knit watch cap running from the front door. The dark hat contrasted sharply with silver hair, matching Patience's description of the Lake Killer. Nash quickly approached the door, weapon in front of him, constantly sweeping the foyer, the doorway and then the front porch. There could be more than one shooter.

A dark beat-up sedan was peeling off onto the suburban street, too far away for Nash to make out the license number. He watched as it turned the corner out of the subdivision, and memorized its profile. He stepped back through the front door, and he pulled the SUV keys out of his pocket.

"Greta, release." He paused to make sure the dog stood up and that Patience followed. Their eyes locked across the great room. "You okay?"

"I'm good. You?"

"Same. I'm going to call this in—stay in here with Greta, away from that back sliding door." He knew that as much as he'd spooked the intruder, if it was the murderer, he'd be likely to circle back and come at the house from the rear. "Do you have a weapon in the house?"

"No, only the one at the clinic."

"Fine. I'll be right back." He was going to have to talk to her about keeping a weapon close by. At least as long as she was targeted by this nutcase.

"Of course." Patience laid her hand on Greta's head. "Want to come help me make some tea, girl?"

Satisfied that they were okay for now, he went out to the K9 vehicle and called in to dispatch. He kept the SUV running in case the assailant returned.

Frank's voice sounded over the hands-free system. Normally cool as a cuke through all kinds of situations, the dispatcher sounded shaken. Everyone at the RRPD adored Patience, and he was no exception. "We'll have a forensic team out there ASAP, Nash."

"I doubt they'll find anything." If there'd been snow or ice on the ground, tire tracks would have been a great lead. But with the streets still dry after the unexpected cold snap, there was little likelihood of any kind of imprint.

"Give me a description of the vehicle again," Frank said.

"Black sedan, late model but a little beat-up, not something you see around here a lot." In this part of South Dakota, folks opted for four-wheel drive, or at least all-wheel drive, especially at this time of year, when a sudden snow squall could leave you stranded without the extra traction power.

"Copy. And, Nash—is our favorite K9 veterinarian okay?"

Nash smiled at Frank's fatherly concern. Everyone at the police department and training center seemed to get that while Patience had a biological family in town, they weren't very loving or close. Fenwick Colton, mayor of Red Ridge and billionaire energy tycoon, had a reputation for treating his children like stock assets. The RRPD knew this and wrapped its arms around their prized veterinarian. The department was its own family.

"She's fine, Frank." As he replied, the reality of what Patience had blurted out just before the gunshot hit him. He could have lost both her and his unborn child with either of those bullets. *It's okay.* Patience and the baby were fine. But Nash's stomach felt as if he'd swallowed a lead weight. He'd just found out he was going to be a father, *was* a father, and it all could have been irrevocably shattered in the blink of an eye.

"Good to hear. You staying with her for now?"

For *now*? Heck, he was in it with Patience for at least the next eighteen years. No, scratch that. He was learning with his half siblings that being a parent wasn't something that would end once they left the house. He'd always care, no matter their ages or places in life.

And now he had a biological child—his son or daughter—to care about. And Patience to work through it with.

"Nash, you there?"

"Yeah, copy that, Frank. I can be reached on my cell phone." He shut the SUV down and stared at the dash. He hated cutting Frank off, but he had to think.

Nothing was going to be the same again. He knew he needed time, but no matter how long it took him to process the news of a baby, and his now permanent attachment to Patience as its father, life went on. The baby was going to be born, and it would need parenting.

He'd been here before, right after his parents had died in that awful car accident. That had been tragic, unexpected, the sorrow reverberating still through him and his siblings with each holiday and school benchmark that passed. Another opportunity to remember his parents would never be there to see the kids graduate, date for the first time, get into college.

Patience being pregnant wasn't tragic. A surprise, sure. A major life change, definitely. But Nash would be damned if he'd let anyone, including a cold-blooded murderer, take from him the joy that the baby would undoubtedly bring.

He wasn't sure how Patience felt about it, but there was no time like the present to ask.

Patience's hands finally stopped trembling as she stroked Greta's thick fur. "You've been through a lot in less than twelve hours, girl."

Greta leaned into her as they sat on the kitchen floor

between the island counter and the sink. They'd gotten up from the living room floor and the dog had sniffed around the entire house until, satisfied they were alone, she'd resumed her protective stance.

Nash didn't have to tell Patience that it had been the murderer who had found her, and wouldn't hesitate to break in via her patio and garden area. She was safest here, behind the kitchen island, away from the line of sight of the sliding door and yard.

Greta's ears perked up and her body stiffened, indicating that Nash was coming back in. Sure enough, Patience heard the front door open and close, his footsteps thudding as he walked over to them. He stood in front of them for a full minute before he spoke to Greta. "Move over, girl."

Greta complied, lying down in the narrow space left, and Nash sank down next to Patience. It would have been too close even five minutes ago, but right now the solid, warm length of his body alongside hers felt good.

"The front door's going to need to be replaced." His voice was low and comforting.

"Is it functional for now?"

"Not really. But I'll get it boarded up. And we need to move you out of here. I know we're both exhausted, but we can't stay here. You won't be able to until we catch the murderer."

"Did you see him? You're sure it was the same guy?"

"He matched your description, at least his height and the color of his hair." Nash's hands were hanging between his bent knees. He lowered one to hers, on the floor, and squeezed. "You're not alone in this, Patience. I'm not going to let anything happen to you or our baby."

She couldn't speak right away. What they'd been through, this latest attack, the enormity of figuring out they were going to be parents—it was all overwhelming.

They sat with his hand over hers, Greta's soft pants filling the silence, for several moments. Patience was beginning to realize that when she was with Nash, time seemed to stand still. When they were together, whatever connection they shared beyond parenthood was uniquely soothing. As if nothing else mattered and she had all the time in the world to get to the next task. Just being with Nash was enough. This wasn't a place she'd been before. Seeking the next career goal, striving to hit the next benchmark were traits she'd gained from her father. With Nash, they didn't seem as urgent.

Finally, her voice returned.

"That was quick—you calling the baby 'ours.'" She shifted her hand out from under his and immediately missed the warmth.

"It—I mean, he or she—*is* ours. I'm in this with you. We need to hash it out, but this isn't the time to talk about it." As if on cue, the siren from the RRPD unit reached them.

She stood up. "I think we're safe for now. That man I saw on the lake is too calculating to come back when he knows the police are here." Yet her hands still shook, and the weight of knowing she was a target zapped her energy.

"We're not done with the baby conversation. First, we have to get you to a place where you'll be safe. Somehow this jerk figured out where you live, so he knows your name. Going to your father's isn't an option, either. He'll find you there."

Which was a relief as far as Patience was concerned. Her dad's autocratic attitude was the last thing she needed. "My father lives in a very secure compound, but you're right, I don't want to put him at risk. Or any of my siblings."

"I'll figure something out."

"You don't have to—I have a place up in the mountains. No one knows about it." She didn't even tell the clinic staff about it. It was her private escape, the one nod to her healthy bank account that she didn't feel bad about. "It's a two-bedroom cabin."

Nash's eyes lit up. "How far away?"

"Twenty miles. A forty-five minute drive on a clear day. It's really up there, with lots of twisty turns." The thought of the drive to her mountain hideaway made her queasy, but that was her pregnancy talking. Mentally, the respite was irresistible. As long as Nash would be there; she didn't want to be alone. "To be honest, I forgot about the length of the drive, or how twisting it is. I'm not so sure I'll enjoy it right now, but we don't have a choice, do we?"

"You're having morning sickness?" Compassion smoothed the rough edges of his voice and his expression was one she wanted to drown in.

"What does a single dude like you know about morning sickness?"

"I remember when my stepmother was pregnant with the kids. I was already thirteen or fourteen when she had the oldest. She'd throw up for, like, the first three months with each baby." He shook his head. "I decided then and there I'd never get a woman pregnant."

"Well, that's a resolution you've busted. And I'm okay. I feel nauseous here and there, but it's not been as bad as I've seen my friends struggle with. Plus, now I'm pretty sure I'm at least twelve if not as much as fourteen weeks pregnant. The worst time for morning sickness has passed."

"I'm so sorry, Patience. I haven't been here for you for any of it."

"I haven't been here for myself! I ignored the symptoms until the last few days." When they'd become impossible to overlook. "If anyone's failed in responsibility to the baby so far, it's me."

"I am an equal partner in this pregnancy." He spoke as though he were taking his oath to be a police officer.

"You didn't mean to get me pregnant. It happens. We were careful." She tried not to think about how careful they'd been, how huge he'd been as she'd rolled the condom over him, begging him to take her again. *Do not look at his crotch.* It would be the ultimate humiliation—trying to console him that this wasn't entirely his fault, as he was taking it, yet coming on to him in such a blatant way.

"But not careful enough." His mouth was a straight line and he stood with his hands on his hips, looking out the kitchen window. She'd expected him to regret that night; he hadn't signed up to be a new father. He had enough with his siblings. No doubt the reality of her pregnancy was hitting him. She decided to let it go for now. Meanwhile, no matter what he said, she wasn't going to have any expectations that he'd be a fully participating father. It was better for her heart to not go there. Nash Maddox was a heart-stopper of the highest caliber.

She nodded at the window, where they could see the patrol unit pulling up in front of her house. "That was quick. I'll make them a pot of coffee."

Nash went out to greet the officers and Patience immediately felt the loss of warmth from his nearness. If her hyperawareness of him affected her this much after only a very long night and part of a day together, how was it going to be when they were holed up at her cabin?

There was no use squelching the thrills that fluttered in her gut, sending heat over her breasts and between her legs. Her desire for Nash was undeniable. And welcome.

Chapter 6

Nash drove to Patience's cabin, and while he had to focus on the treacherous road, he couldn't ignore how much he enjoyed being in her company. They'd both been awake for over twenty-four hours and yet her nearness buoyed him. Why hadn't he followed up with her after their one-nighter? It shouldn't have taken a murder investigation and danger to Patience to bring them together again.

"You weren't kidding when you said your place is way up here. I don't think I've ever ventured to this part of the mountain before." Which was saying a lot, since he'd camped and hunted and ran roughshod with the best of them while he was growing up. As an only child for almost fourteen years, Nash had had his father indulging his every whim. Even after his parents divorced and his dad remarried and had four kids in his new family, he'd always made time for Nash.

"I picked it on purpose." Her voice was stretched thin, but he couldn't look at her to see why as he made a hairpin turn around the mountain. The shoulder was nonexistent and he'd guess the drop-off was at least two hundred feet.

"This might be fate, you know. We need to get to know one another better if we're raising a kid together. It's clear neither of us wanted to make the first move toward a relationship after our night together." *Crap.* His thoughts had turned to words before he engaged his mental filter. He was going to tick her off before they even got to the cabin.

"You don't need to stay with me, Nash. Leave me an extra weapon if you want to, but no one else knows about this place, save for my family. I'm safe here."

Back on a straight stretch of road, he risked a glance at her. Her eyes were closed, her hand hanging on to the overhead handle of his personal Jeep for dear life. "If you think you're going to throw up, I can pull over." He couldn't look at her for as long as he wanted—the road was taking them around another particularly tricky switchback. He heard Greta shift in the back and silently thanked the dog for her steadfastness.

"Just. Keep. Going." Spoken through gritted teeth, yet with steel. He couldn't help but smile. Patience was nothing if she wasn't tough as nails. One of her many qualities that attracted him to her.

"I'll bet the views here are spectacular when it's not so overcast." They'd entered some low-lying clouds, making the trip seem all the more mysterious. Clandestine. The highway evened out, but he still drove with care, as there was barely a shoulder on either side of the road. He knew it was deceptive—the woods made it look like there was level ground right off the paved road, but a sheer cliff was just beyond the trees.

"They are spectacular." Her eyes opened and a bit of color came back into her cheeks. "We're almost there. Take the next left and pull up to the gate. I'll give you the code."

"I'm impressed that you have security up here."

"It was a compromise with my father. I needed to use a portion of my trust fund as collateral to buy and upgrade this place, and he agreed only after I promised to put in top-notch security. Not many people know about it—my family is all."

"I like your father's thinking on this one." Although he wasn't a fan of Fenwick Colton, the pompous ass who basically controlled the county's—and therefore the RRPD's—purse strings, Nash appreciated that the man cared enough about his daughter to insist on the security measures.

"I'm not so sure it was about my safety as much as his pride. He's never gotten over me paying my way through college and vet school, and I've since paid back every penny of what I borrowed from him for this cabin."

"I had no idea you'd done that—paid for your schooling." He'd assumed her father took care of it.

"Most people believe I didn't, but that's okay. I didn't do it for anyone but me."

Within minutes he pulled up to a large gate, blanketed on either side by dense forest and a lethal rock outcropping that rose to high cliffs. They were in a valley of sorts, which made it feel like a fortress. "I don't see the keypad."

"Because there isn't one." She had her phone out and was tapping on it. "It's app-driven. I control it all with my phone."

"Any chance I can have that code, or whatever I need?"

"We'll set your phone up once we're in the cabin."

The deceptively rustic gate swung open and he drove them onto the graveled road, which after about another mile led to what appeared to be a modest, almost run-down cabin.

"And we're here." Patience was out of the passenger seat in a blink, her long legs practically loping up to the quaint porch. Chairs, a rocker and a couple tables made it appear well used.

"You spend a lot of time on this porch, don't you?"

She cast him a shy smile. "I do. Layla comes up with me sometimes, but other than that, it's all mine."

"So the phone unlocks your door, too?"

"Yes." An audible click sounded from the front door and he followed her into the cabin. Greta entered in turn and immediately plopped herself on the largest area of open floor, in front of the fireplace. Greta always sought out the coolest place in any dwelling, as her bulk kept her body temperature high. Patience laughed and he liked the sound of it. She visibly relaxed, the tension in her face easing as they walked around the cozy space.

"Patience, please know I'm here to protect you. You're safe."

She shot him a sharp look. "I know. Why are you saying that?"

"You've been wound tight since you saw the murder. That's understandable, but you don't have to carry that worry. Let me do it for you."

"You're not the one with the target on your back." Her sharp reply communicated her fear.

"True. But if you can't totally let it go, at least let me shoulder some of it with you." It was tricky convincing her to trust him. So far he'd failed at keeping the murderer from coming after her. And then there was the pregnancy; she hadn't wound up pregnant on her own. He owed her at least a sense of personal safety.

"Fair enough." She turned toward the kitchen area and he followed.

The cabin was rustic in all the right places—the log walls, river-stone fireplace and chimney, a cast-iron teakettle on the six-burner gas stove. But it was a fully modernized home, too. Granite counters and a solid butcher block–covered island, stainless steel kitchen appliances. Even the fireplace, as authentic as it was, had a gas insert.

"Go ahead and flick on the fire if you want. It'll take the chill out of the room. The top switch is for the flames and the bottom for the fan, to circulate it through the great room."

Nash hit the switches and watched the fire ignite.

"Not what you expected?" She spoke from the kitchen, but she must have been watching his reaction, his smile when, with a touch of his finger, the old-fashioned country fireplace lit up as if he'd stoked it all night.

"When you said *cabin*, I envisioned something more plain, quite frankly."

"Trust me, this was all that when I purchased it. The kitchen and back bedrooms are the only original parts of the building. I had the front wall knocked out to create the great room area, and added on the porch. Before, it served as no more than a hunter's hideaway."

"How did you find it?"

"While I was in vet school in California, I used to keep an eye on rural homes in this area. I always intended to return to Red Ridge, even though my father never believed me. He thought that once I lived in California long enough I'd never want to come back here."

"Why did you come back?"

She regarded him. The midday sun reflected in her eyes and brought out the amber sparks. The rich color belied the shadows under her eyes, and a sharp pang of guilt hit him. The mother of his future child needed to rest.

"My calling is to heal animals. I've known it since I was a very young child. For a while I wasn't sure if I could do it." As he stared at her, silent, she went on, "Animals have been my solace throughout my life. My parents had a volatile relationship, and after my mother died, my father had a slew of women he dated, some more seriously than others. As I'm sure you know, he married and divorced several times. It made life unpleasant, depending upon the wife. Our dogs and horses kept me going. I knew I'd only be happy if I could work with animals as an adult."

It was easy to imagine her as a young girl, with the same big brown eyes and flame-touched caramel hair. "Before I had to take care of my brothers and sisters, I wouldn't have appreciated what you're telling me as much. I understand now how much kids value security, routine." He swallowed around the perplexing lump that had formed in his throat. "I'm glad you had your pets to help you through it." The thought of any of his siblings having to search for love from an animal instead of their parents or him made him ache. And feel angry for Patience's sake at the same time.

"It wasn't just my pets. They were wonderful, and pets are great companions. But I love them all—farm, domestic, wild. All animals fill my soul."

"Even the bears?"

She grinned. "Yeah. Even the bears. Although I don't have any desire to run into one out here. I keep a bull-horn by the front door for that reason."

"To scare them off." He thought it was ingenious, but would feel better if she had a weapon. "You know, a rifle—"

She held up both hands. "Hold it. I get that you're law enforcement and used to being around firearms. I'm not antigun, in that way. Around these parts, we all learn to use rifles early on for good reason. And it's not that I'm against having a rifle out here to protect myself from bears and the occasional mountain lion. I just don't need one. I haven't ever come close to being targeted by an animal on this mountain. The bears pass through every spring, and I'm always extra careful to make a lot of noise so that I never surprise a mama or her cubs. And you know as well as I do that there's enough wildlife and plants to support them. They don't have to come after me or try to break into the cabin for a meal."

"It's just that...you have more than yourself to consider now."

She wiped her eyes with her hands and her shoulders sagged in exhaustion. Guilt gut punched him.

"I'm sorry, Patience. You need rest." As did he, but he wasn't carrying their child. "Mind if I look around the rest of the place? Why don't you go get a hot shower, then settle in to sleep?"

"I don't mind at all. Go ahead, make yourself at home. A shower sounds good. There's actually two showers, so don't hesitate to take one yourself if you'd like. I've installed a flash heater so the hot water never runs out."

"Thanks. I'll take you up on that." Later, after he was certain she was asleep. He'd post Greta on guard at the front door.

While Patience showered, he poked around inside and outside the cabin. Built on a solid rock-and-concrete foundation, it was impenetrable except through the front door and the bedroom windows. There was a loft above the great room where she'd set up a technically up-to-date office. It also had a sleeper sofa, and provided an eagle's-eye view of the front door. It would be the perfect place for him to bunk, with Greta taking the ground floor.

Getting to Red Ridge each morning was going to be

trickier and, in all truth, a pain. They'd have to budget their time and coordinate shifts. Because no way was he going to let Patience commute on her own. He was going to stick to her like pine tar in June until they caught the killer.

He pulled his phone out to call the kids and see how his aunt and uncle were managing. The thing was, he hadn't thought much at all about his siblings until now. He knew they were safe and well taken care of. He was more worried about Patience and what all this stress was doing to the baby.

And if he were really being honest with himself, he wasn't convinced he'd be able to stay under the same roof as her without touching her again. Being around her roused his desire, and it wasn't something he could boil down to basic horniness or physical need. He was hot for one woman, and she happened to be naked under the shower just one flight of stairs down from the loft he stood in.

This was going to be a challenging mission.

Patience had never felt more tired than she did as the hot water massaged her neck and shoulders. She'd wanted a long hot bath and had a soaking tub to do it in, but was too worn-out to contemplate filling it. And she couldn't risk falling asleep in the water. Not that the constant nagging sensation of being stalked would allow it. Nash had taken evasive measures to ensure they weren't followed, and it made sense that the killer would lie low for a while, until the hunt for him wasn't so intense. Maybe she could catch a few hours of sleep.

If she wasn't so tired she would have giggled at Nash's expression when he saw the cabin, especially the interior. Layla had reacted the same way when she'd first seen the transformation Patience made. As much as she'd paid for every single cent of her education, including vet school, she'd not felt an iota of guilt for taking the loan out and making the cabin exactly how she wanted it. Her pay was excellent and it wasn't as though she needed it to feed a family. So she'd sunk her first earnings into the cabin.

Thinking about her paycheck reminded her that her father had mentioned that future funding for the K9 clinic wasn't a guarantee. It had been a huge part of the family blowup they'd had right before her fateful night with Nash. Layla had assured her that the clinic remained a top priority of Colton Energy, and that Layla's fiancé would solve everything.

Patience shut off the shower and reached for a towel. How she and Layla had both come from the same DNA was beyond her. They were close and loved one another, but her sister put money and business ahead of all else in her life. Layla's agreement to remain engaged to smarmy Hamlin Harrington was a clue that she cared more about Colton Energy than herself.

Patience dried off and put on the long johns she kept at the cabin. Her stomach, which she hadn't even thought twice about before she took the pregnancy test yesterday, was definitely more pronounced, but not so much that it affected her stretchy clothes. Yet. Her scrubs and workout clothes were more forgiving, but no way could she squeeze into her favorite jeans. She ran her hand over her belly, musing over the fact that an entire human being grew in there.

She sat on her bed, thinking about getting a cup of hot tea before she turned in. But fighting her comfy surroundings was too much.

The wrought iron bed frame that she'd found in an antiques store in Sioux Falls and painted white offset the fluffy comforter and pillows with her favorite floral pattern. She knew she needed to talk to Nash more, reassure him that it was totally okay with her that he wasn't interested in being a father, but sleep beckoned.

As she slid between her flannel sheets, the last thing she thought about was phoning the clinic when she woke up, to check on her patients. Especially Fred. That made her mind flash to the cold, heartless eyes of the killer, and his voice calling out, "Where are you, you bitch?" as he stormed the building. But even that didn't keep her awake.

Nash heard the complete silence settle on the cabin like a down blanket not long after the water stopped. He shoved aside any sense of politeness or healthy boundaries as he went and checked to make sure Patience was okay. Her form was still under a mound of covers in the decidedly feminine master bedroom. It was a grown-up version of the room Maeve and Paige shared, which they'd decorated before their parents died.

Patience was down for the count, or at least for several hours, so he put a cup of decaf coffee on to brew, thanks to the ultramodern machine in the kitchen, and took Greta for a quick walk on the property. They'd missed dinner, but sleep was more important at this point. The surrounding woods were dense and definitely a deterrent to a casual trespasser, hunting or hiking. Nothing was impenetrable to a professional criminal, however, and Nash's instinct told him the murderer was definitely experienced. He hadn't handled many murder cases in his decade-long career, but the Groom Killer had changed that. Nash had seen enough lately to know that the lake murder was no random event. Nor was the way the bad guy had tried to dispose of the victim.

Nash's phone buzzed as he came back to the house and he took the call from Finn.

"Sir. Maddox speaking."

"Nash, I want to thank you and Greta for your hard work last night and this morning. How's our favorite K9 veterinarian doing?" Chief Colton had ordered Nash to stay with Patience until they caught the Lake Killer.

"She's doing better, sound asleep at the moment. We're at her private cabin, about forty minutes out from Red Ridge. I'll be commuting in with her until the coast is clear."

"Sounds like a plan. We're going to need you and Greta when we comb the lake for any other unknown victims. It's already getting too late to go in and do it properly today, and I'm not sure about tomorrow, as we have to wait on the state unit to back us up, but we'll be set within forty-eight hours. Get some rest and we'll see you by daybreak."

"Yes, sir." He made a mental note to check out his dive gear, which he kept in a locker at the RRPD.

They disconnected. Nash retrieved his coffee from

the kitchen, noting that the house was still peacefully silent. Good. Patience needed the sleep.

Greta raised her head from her front paws to look at him when he stepped back out onto the porch. She'd taken up almost half the space, obviously needing her rest, too. But she'd never be fully asleep, he knew. Greta always had at least one ear listening for trouble.

"You're a good girl, Greta. Chief says good job for yesterday." He rubbed the top of her head and behind her ears as she languidly thumped her tail against the wooden floor.

He sighed as he sat and put his feet up on the porch railing, settling into the rocking chair with the cup of coffee he'd made. Seeing Patience's flowery room reminded him of the girls, and then the boys. All four were fine and had made it to school, according his aunt and uncle. He wished he could let any worry for them go, but it was impossible.

The girls were seventeen and fifteen. Paige would be out of the house and in college this time next year. It was early in her senior year, but all indications were that she'd be getting into her first choice—Pennsylvania State. She wanted to go away, and while he supported all the kids in going to whatever schools they could get into, he wished she'd picked a place like Sioux Falls. As hard as the past few years had been, he'd grown attached to his siblings more than he'd ever dreamed. He was going to miss her. And it wouldn't be long before Maeve would follow on her heels. She'd already begun to apply to the US Naval Academy in Annapolis, Maryland. She wanted to be a navy fighter pilot.

At least the younger two—Troy and Jon, twelve and thirteen—were going to keep him busy as they grew from boys to young men. With them being complete opposites, he often had to juggle taking them to either Jon's soccer team practices or Troy's card games at the local game store. Both wanted to go to college some-day, but for different reasons. Jon wanted to earn a full-ride athletic scholarship and become a sports jour-nalist. Troy wanted to develop video games. If Nash could harness their combined energy and abilities, it'd pay for all four kids' college and graduate school ex-penses. He smiled as he looked out on the dozens of tall fir trees that guarded the cabin.

The serenity lulled him and he actually felt the ten-sion drain out of his frame for the first time in days. But the chill in the air wasn't conducive to napping, and besides, he needed solid downtime. He stood and stretched.

"Come on, Greta. You can keep watch from inside."

He'd have to ignore the constant pull of Patience's presence from her bedroom, the hum of awareness in the air whenever she was around. Otherwise he'd never get to sleep.

Chapter 7

Patience woke up in a darkened room, and from her smart watch saw that it was almost morning. She'd slept straight through the night. The October days were getting shorter and shorter, and under the canopy of the mountain forest it was more pronounced.

She slipped out of the bed and donned sweatpants and a hoodie over her long underwear, needing the extra layers. It was time to light up the heater.

Only after she pulled socks on did she remember everything. The shock of finding out she was pregnant. The murderer dumping his victim into a frigid lake as if he were throwing garbage over the side. Her frantic call to dispatch. Nash.

Nash.

She leaned on the door frame before she left her

room, forcing herself to take several deep breaths. It was a calming technique they all learned during stress-management training at the RRPD or at the K9 clinic. And usually it worked. The slight tremble she felt, no matter how calm the moment, was caused by something she couldn't help. The worry of being killed, of course. That wasn't going to ease up until the Lake Killer was apprehended.

Her attraction to Nash wasn't letting up anytime soon, either. And he was here with her.

"Let it go." She forcefully expelled air, trying to clear her mind as she emptied her lungs.

The cabin's sense of security enveloped her. She padded as softly as possible down the short corridor to the kitchen and great room. Nash had to be sleeping; he'd looked exhausted before she'd gone in for her shower. She stopped in the kitchen, pushed the heat button on the thermostat and set a pot of coffee to brew.

The silhouette of Greta's great head drew her attention to the far wall, under the large picture window that had been part of the cabin's renovation three years ago. Greta faced the window as she monitored the porch and woods, but looked over her hulking shoulder to acknowledge Patience's arrival.

Patience offered the dog a grin before she put her finger to her lips. She looked up at the loft and saw Nash's form was stretched out along the leather sofa, a thin throw over his torso and thighs. He hadn't even unfolded the sleeper into a bed. She stifled a giggle at the length of his frame on the couch, and went back down the hall to the guest room, where she yanked the comforter off the double bed.

Her intention was to cover Nash with the much more substantial blanket, but she paused once she'd crept up the steps to the loft, loath to wake him. She stood in front of the sofa, the thick down throw in her arms.

He looked so peaceful in sleep. Definitely Nash, and unquestionably masculine, but serene. His face was smooth, with no indication of the lines that often stamped it during the day. There was no sign of the professional hard-ass she'd witnessed in action last night, or early this morning. Nash Maddox was 100 percent male. She let her gaze drift over him, his form only half-concealed by the afghan her sister had crocheted. She paused her observation where his T-shirt rode up, exposing rock-hard abs covered with dark hair. Her breath caught and she let the thrill of sexual awareness run through her. His stomach teased her, shooting a pang of longing through her as she fought to keep her fingers from reaching out and—

"Are you going to keep staring at me, or give me some warmth?"

Patience jumped in surprise with a squeal. He opened one eye, his mouth curving.

She dumped the blanket on him. "There you go." But instead of leaving him be, she sank down onto the floor. "You know, this is a sleeper sofa. You didn't have to be so uncomfortable all night. Why didn't you take the guest room?"

"I need to have an uninterrupted sight line to the front door."

"Oh." Of course. He took his job seriously, protecting her. She looked down from the loft and saw Greta had moved to lean up against the oak door, a definite hindrance to anyone trying to enter the cabin. "It looks like Greta knows her business."

He rubbed his eyes and sat up, dragging the blankets with him. "Greta, at ease." When Greta cocked her head, as if trying to figure out why he was releasing her from her post, he added, "You're a good dog. Jeez, it's freezing in here."

"I fixed that. I turned on the heater on my way up here." She was in long johns and a heavy bathrobe, but he'd slept in…his underwear from what she could see. She noticed his grin. "What's so funny?"

"You. In a good way. This is the most rustic setting for a cabin and yet you've managed to outfit it with the latest in technology and convenience."

"If you're expecting me to apologize for that, don't hold your breath." She leaned her back against the sofa. Greta stood up, stretched and slowly climbed up the loft stairs. The huge dog placed her head in Patience's lap, and she buried her fingers in the thick, dark fur. "She is the biggest snuggle bug, aren't you, Greta?"

"Did you get enough sleep?" Nash asked.

She turned to look at him and his eyes blazed across the short distance between them. She glanced away. It was too easy to think he was looking at her with more than professional interest. She peered into Greta's liquid black eyes instead.

"Yes, thank you. I don't know the last time I went that long without sleeping. Do you realize we'd been awake for the better part of twenty-four hours by the time we got here?"

He chuckled, the sound low and sexy. "I sure do. Man, am I glad that my aunt and uncle are with the kids. I love my brothers and sisters, but it's nice to have to only worry about work, too."

"That's fair." Besides the constant sexual tension, the silent topic of the baby hung between them and she wondered when he'd talk about it again. If he'd mention the baby on his own.

"Is there coffee?"

"Yes, I'm sorry—in the kitchen, on the counter. I made a whole pot, but if you don't like regular dark roast there's a single-cup maker there, too. Help yourself."

He stood and she did, too, ignoring the part of her that wished she'd woken him up with something other than coffee. As he meandered down to the kitchen with the blanket wrapped around him she followed, as did Greta. She didn't see any skin but his muscular calves. Was it the baby hormones that made her want to touch said calves and maybe get more of a peek of what was under his blanket?

They stopped in the kitchen and she was transfixed by how much he filled the space. His scent overrode the coffee aroma and she had to remind herself for the umpteenth time that her sexual journey with Nash had ended almost three months ago.

"Are you able to have full caffeine? I mean, is the baby? Patience?" Damn it, he'd caught her staring and was making fun of her.

"I'm not in some kind of daze, you know."

He shrugged and then dug in the cabinet for a mug. He chose a dark green ceramic one she'd received gratis from a veterinary drug company. The most masculine cup in her cabinet. Of course he did. She couldn't blame him for being such a guy, but then again, he was. So. Incredibly. Hot.

Frustrated, she left the kitchen and took a seat in the living room's easy chair, next to the sofa.

"Patience?"

She shook her head. "I'm still a little groggy, I suppose. I don't usually sleep for twelve hours."

"Is it grogginess, Patience?" He padded into the living room with his cup of black coffee and sat on the sofa. When he leaned forward, his knees were a scant inch from hers, and his scent again transported her back to their night together.

"Nash, I'm not looking for a relationship any more than you are. We'd agreed that our night, that one night, was a onetime deal. I don't expect anything more from you. Honest."

"What if I'm looking for more? What would you say then?"

"That you're only doing this because of the baby. And in case I didn't make it clear, I'm raising it on my own. I won't ever ask you for anything. I told you because it was the right thing to do." She prided herself on always keeping things aboveboard. It was how she'd kept her identity as a child in a family of billionaires and the accompanying lifestyle.

"If you think for one minute that I'm going to say

okay to the Patience Plan, you don't know me very well."

She knew him enough, though. "You're already raising four kids."

"I am. And the two oldest will be out the door to college within the next two years, one right after the other. The boys could benefit from having a baby brother or sister. Nothing better for teenage birth control than seeing the responsibilities that come with a child."

"We didn't set a very good example. I mean, with the birth control part."

"So the condom didn't work. They usually do. And to be honest, were we as careful as we could have been? I saw you down at least two champagne cocktails that evening, and I know I had a few beers. Not that drinking is an excuse."

"But it sure let our inhibitions down." As soon as she said it, she grimaced. "Sorry. I tend to forget my mental filter when I'm tired. To be truthful, I would have done it all stone-cold sober." And she would have. She wasn't under the influence of anything now but the nearness of Nash, and she wanted to jump his bones.

"You've said nothing but the truth." He leaned over and placed his cup on the coffee table. But instead of settling back onto the sofa, he got down on his knees and placed his hands on hers, their faces level.

Patience's breathing slowed as her heartbeat sped up. It was as if they were in their own sensual bubble whenever he was around, and certainly when he got this close to her. She knew she should at least grasp at a semblance of professionalism, show him that she wasn't the same woman he'd been with that night. But she was that woman, and more.

"Nash."

He raised his brows very slightly and inclined his head, making his intent clear. But he wouldn't follow through until she said yes.

Instead, she closed the distance between them and kissed him first. His lips were firm but so soft, and at the smallest flicker of her tongue he opened his mouth to her. Patience let the chaos of the last two days go as she gave in to her need.

Nash's arms came up and he cupped her head, more firmly sealing his mouth over hers. They parried for the lead, their tongues waging battle, and she remembered at once why they'd been so good together.

So good it had made a baby.

She pulled back.

"What?" His eyes were still closed and he landed a kiss on her jawline, her throat.

"Nash, we've already agreed that last time was—"

She groaned as he kissed his way back to her lips. *Just a little more*, she promised herself. When his tongue filled her mouth, she wasn't sure why she'd ever resisted him.

Nash didn't allow himself to think of anything but the taste of Patience's lips as they continued to kiss like sex-starved teenagers. He wasn't going to suggest they go to bed again since he didn't have any condoms with him. But there were other ways to please her. He paused, pulled back from the kiss reluctantly, looked into her very liquid brown eyes.

"I want to taste you again, Patience. All of you." She answered him by shimmying out of her pajama bottoms and long johns, throwing off her hoodie as if they were in a cabana on a tropical beach and not in a cabin in the mountains.

Her heavy-lidded eyes opened far enough for him to see her want, her need. "Nash." She breathed his name as if she'd come to the end of a long search.

He knew he had. The taste of her lips, her skin, made him need more. Her moans and sighs guided his tongue, told him what she liked best, what turned her on.

His erection strained against his boxer briefs, but this wasn't about his release—this was all for Patience. He kissed his way down over her rounded abdomen, where he dipped his tongue into the indentation of her belly button. She cried out in need and he chuckled. "Not so fast, babe. Enjoy each—" he licked her hip bone "—and every—" he sucked on the skin just above her bikini panties "—bit." He kissed her through the flimsy fabric, purposefully blowing his breath into her, the satisfaction of making her squirm in response filling him with something he couldn't name.

She helped him get her panties off, then lay on the sofa, her legs spread wide. Nash paused, stunned by her beauty.

"Don't make me beg, Nash."

He worked his way back up her legs to the insides of her thighs, taking his time, leaving wet kisses where he knew she liked them. He'd memorized her every response and preference that night they'd shared, and still there was so much more to learn about her. He wanted to know all of Patience.

Every last bit.

Patience delighted in the contrast of the cool sofa beneath her and the white-hot heat of Nash's mouth on the insides of her thighs. Her nipples tightened, as taut as the need she had for this man.

For Nash.

"Don't stop, Nash. Please."

"Babe." He placed his mouth over her sex and swirled his tongue over her most intimate parts, swollen for him. Because of him. Her entire body was inflamed, aware only of Nash's skillful lovemaking and her urgency for release. She tried to hang on, to make it last, but like the relationship building between them, and the unborn child that they'd made, her response kept growing.

The initial waves of her climax began, and when Nash slid one, then two fingers inside her, the internal counterpressure catapulted her into a strong, breath-stealing orgasm. Her cries echoed about the cabin and she gasped for breath. As soon as she came down from the climax, Nash surprised her. Instead of stopping, he kept going, kept stroking and licking until she came again. And again.

He didn't let up until she begged him to.

Nash looked at her, his eyes glazed with the same feelings she had—but how could this be? He hadn't enjoyed the release she had.

"Babe, I can do this all day."

"I could let you, but I want to please you, too. While I still have the strength." She laughed then, a long, low rumble that reflected the depth of her sexual satisfaction.

"This was for you, Patience." He sat up and gently covered her with the blanket. "You're going to get cold."

She sat up and sidled closer. "Never. Not next to you."

He shook with his need for her and fought his instinct to move over her, to take her fully and completely. He wanted her so badly. He'd savored every last lick, every last taste of her. And still he wanted more.

"We don't need to use a condom anymore. I'm already pregnant. As long as you're clean? You said you were that night."

"As did you. And yes, I'm clean. But, Patience, we don't have to do this. We moved so quickly last time."

"By agreement." She leaned over and kissed him. The kiss was sexy and full of both their scents, with her musk still on his lips. Her hands reached down and stroked him, and he stopped worrying about consequences. He needed Patience, had to be inside her.

He stood up and they both got him out of his T-shirt and briefs. Patience grasped his buttocks and without preamble took him in her mouth. Her tongue teased and flirted before her lips closed around him with the perfect amount of pressure.

"Babe." He stroked her lush, sexy hair, held her to him as long as he dared. Reluctantly, he gently pulled back.

She looked up at him, puzzlement in her eyes. "Tell me, Nash. What do you want?"

He eased her back and lowered himself over her. She opened her legs again, this time to receive him. "As much as I love your mouth on my cock, I need to be inside you."

"Then do it, Nash. Take me."

He prayed there'd be another time to take it slowly, to spend all day and night with her. But not now. He entered her in one swift stroke and groaned with the sheer ecstasy of her tight heat wrapped around him.

"I've missed this, Patience." He began to move, and her hips met his as she gasped in pleasure. He didn't know where or when, but they became one, seeking a common goal: totally unity.

His climax came at him like a Mack truck on an empty highway, with little warning before the huge spasm of total abandonment hit.

This…this was what had been missing from his life. Not the sex, not the release, but the completion with Patience.

They lay together, Nash atop her, for several minutes as they both caught their breaths. Came down to earth. Only when Patience's thoughts turned back to why they were here in the cabin together did she nudge Nash to sit. As soon as he left her she missed him, and he was only inches away. But the omnipresent fear of being killed chased away her afterglow.

She stood and ran her fingers through her hair. Hair that his fingers had turned into an unholy mess. She couldn't keep the grin from her face. It'd been worth it.

Except now they had to face reality again. Only after she'd increased the distance between them by several feet and two easy chairs did she stop and face him.

"Nash, we're playing with fire here. With our emotions. There's no future for us, and we'd both do best to stick to our original agreement." She watched him as he stood and wrapped the blanket around himself. A pity, as his naked body was heaven-sent.

"Plans change, Patience. We weren't planning on you getting pregnant. Yet you are." Nash's face revealed no frustration, no recrimination. Just openness, honesty.

"Of course, we didn't plan for the baby. But facts are facts." She didn't like it that they couldn't be friends with benefits, either. This time had been a mistake. But it didn't feel like a mistake to her body. In fact, she'd never felt so at ease with a man as she did with Nash.

That enough was reason to guard her heart.

Patience looked at him, her hair mussed from their lovemaking, and it was all he could do to not kiss her again, let the desire build until they were making love on every surface in the cabin.

He stood, naked under the blanket he'd wrapped around himself. "I need to shower. When I come back, we're going sit down and hash this out."

But when he came back into the kitchen, after a quick shower and putting his jeans and flannel shirt on, the time to talk had passed. Patience was engrossed in a phone conversation and pointed at the fresh coffeepot as she spared him a quick glance.

He helped himself to a large mugful and added in some of the milk she had in her fridge. It was almond milk, but it would do. Paige had taken to almond milk the last year and he had to admit it wasn't the worst thing on the planet. He looked out the kitchen window and saw two deer meandering through the trees out back. The kids would love this cabin.

Crap. When he was with Patience it was easy to lose track of time. He needed to check on them. He took Greta with him and let himself out the side door.

"Hey, Uncle Jim. How are you and Aunt Clara doing?"

"We're great, the kids are fine. Paige and Maeve helped us get the boys out the door on time. Those two will fiddle about all morning, won't they?"

Nash laughed. "Yes, they will, but don't take any guff from them."

"Oh, they're polite. They just like to sleep a lot. I remember feeling tired when I was their age, but sleeping in was never an option." Uncle Jim and Nash's mother had been raised on a cattle ranch and had been expected to perform their share of chores from a young age.

"They're not having the same upbringing as you and Mom did, that's for sure."

"That's okay. It's not a bad thing to be able to be a kid a little longer. How's your case going?"

"I don't know—I'm about to head back into town and check it out for myself. I'm going to be on this assignment until we catch the bad guy. He's threatened our K9 vet twice. Greta and I are keeping an eye on her."

"I didn't realize your duties included bodyguard."

"They don't, not normally. But since Patience Colton is the department's K9 veterinarian, I've stepped up. The RRPD takes care of its own."

"I hear you. Dr. Colton took care of Sleepy, you know." Uncle Jim referred to the cocker spaniel he and Aunt Clara had had for almost fifteen years. They'd never had kids of their own and the little dog had been like a child to them. They'd had to put her down last spring after a cancer diagnosis.

"I didn't realize Patience was the vet who'd cared for Sleepy." He remembered his aunt and uncle's ordeal over the dog when it took ill, and how they'd brought it into Red Ridge after hearing about the K9 clinic being open to civilian patients, but he hadn't connected the dots.

"Dr. Colton was, and is, excellent at her job. She was also single at the time and very attractive." Uncle Jim was as subtle as a landslide.

"She is still both, in fact." Nash wasn't going to pussyfoot around it.

"Does that have anything to do with why you've taken such an interest in her safety?" Uncle Jim's voice had the same positive inflection his mother's had had. A sharp pang of grief tugged deep in Nash's chest.

His first instinct was to blow Uncle Jim off and make light of his query. But the man who'd helped Nash piece his and the kids' lives back together deserved more. Besides, Uncle Jim knew him well and would know he was lying.

"Yeah, it does. But don't say anything to Aunt Clara for now. I don't know how it'll go and I don't want to get her hopes up." Aunt Clara had done everything but hold a rally in downtown Red Ridge and Sioux Falls to find a woman for Nash. She was certain that the right partner would make his time raising the kids go more quickly, and help Nash through his grief.

She hadn't been wrong; his night with Patience had underscored to him how lonely he'd been. And how downright horny he was. Except his sexual needs and fantasies were always centered around Patience, ever since he'd started working more closely with her at the K9 clinic. As if their attraction to one another had always been there and only waited for the perfect time—the night after their last K9 training workshop—to come to the surface.

And now they were going to have a baby together.

"You still there, Nash?"

"Yeah, just checking on Greta. We're out walking through the woods."

"I imagine it's beautiful up on that mountain."

"It is, but again, please don't mention it to anyone. I've got to keep her here safe and sound until we know it's clear for her to go back to her home in Red Ridge."

"No worries there. Don't you worry about the kids, Nash. They're older and understand your responsibility to the community. Just do your job and we'll all be waiting for you when it's done."

"Thanks so much, Uncle Jim."

He disconnected the call and looked around the cabin's

perimeter for any signs of a prowler who'd come while he and Patience had slept. And made love. As cunning as the murderer was, Nash had learned over the years that someone being where he or she shouldn't always left a trace. It was very difficult for a human being to leave zero evidence behind.

"Greta, work." He moved her through the task of sniffing around the cabin and surrounding woods, but she never alerted to anything unusual. He was confident that she'd tell him if she smelled anything from the boat the man had used to dump the body.

Nash heard the door open and watched as Patience came outside. Her eyes were bright and her cheeks had the color of ripe peaches. Her rest had done her good. He shouldn't feel the resulting swirl of satisfaction over something so simple. Sure, he was here to help keep her safe, but he'd not been the one to make her sleep. It was just the paternal connection; he was happy the mother of his future child was doing better.

It couldn't totally be due to how hard she'd come in his arms.

"I need to go to the clinic." Patience walked up to him. They watched Greta sniff through a pile of dried pine needles. Nash called her to his side, where she dutifully sat.

"We can leave now, if you'd like. I have to head in to the station, and you do, too—you need to give your description to the sketch artist."

"I want to bring my car back here, Nash. I can't be tied to you forever." And yet she was. She carried his child. When would this new reality stop taking his breath away?

"It's not safe for you to go back and forth on your own. Not yet. And the killer knows your vehicle and will follow you here in a heartbeat."

"If he's still around. Don't you think he may have taken off for now? He has to know the entire county, the state even, is looking for him."

"That may be true, but I'm not willing to take any chances, Patience."

Her chin rose in what he knew was her unconscious signal that she wasn't going to bend. "I have choices here, Nash. Being pregnant doesn't change that."

Their eyes met, and besides the instant zing to his crotch that always accompanied eye contact with her, he felt something different. Something that they were building together.

Trust.

He shook his head. "I'm sorry, Patience. You're as knowledgeable as I am about this case at this point. And it's totally your call as to whether we travel together or solo. But you can't blame me for having an added interest, can you? You're pregnant with my baby."

"A baby I told you I don't expect you to help me with." Her gaze softened a notch. "Although I guess I haven't been too understanding. You've had a lot to process these last hours, too."

"Let's get to the station while the sketch artist is still there." Keeping to the business at hand suited him best.

He'd thought he wanted to have a heart-to-heart with her about how they'd handle raising the baby together, but she was right. He needed some time to process.

Chapter 8

Glad that Nash had to focus on the road back into town, Patience used the time for self-examination. Something about him made her words come out ahead of her thoughts. She wasn't used to curbing her usual forthright manner, or having to engage her mental filter so much.

In her family and at the clinic, she was pragmatic, and prided herself on speaking her mind. It made life easier for all. The emotional tug-of-war she felt whenever she was around Nash called for a different tactic, and worst of all, her namesake. She needed to be more patient with Nash. He'd only just found out he was going to be a father, and hadn't had time to come to terms with the ramifications. Instead of being free to be a bachelor in six years as he deserved, when his youngest brother came of age, he'd have to start the clock over the minute the baby was born.

Her baby. She couldn't think about it as theirs, or about his paternity, without her emotions taking her to dangerous places. To a life where she'd have a partner to share everything with, including the joy of raising a child together.

"You're awfully quiet." Nash was barreling down the mountain road, obviously as eager as she was to be back in civilization. Greta sat in the rear, her canine seat belt keeping her almost one hundred fifty pounds from flying into the front between their seats.

"I'm trying to remember the exact details of the murderer's face, so that I don't mess up with the artist."

"You can't mess up. Just tell her what you saw, and you'll know right away if her drawing matches."

"You're right." It was easier, safer to talk to Nash about work. "How long before we catch him, do you think?"

She watched his profile as he made the turn onto the highway that was a straight shot into Red Ridge. "No telling. He's a professional, that much is clear. And I'm not a detective, so I'm not privy to all the details on the case, not as they happen. Unless it pertains to your safety. You know as much as I do. We can ask for a recap when we get there."

"That would be good. That should take about an hour, right? I do have to go by the clinic at some point today, Nash."

"It's too risky."

"Hear me out. You can drive me there in a police

vehicle. I'll wear a ski cap and borrow your jacket. I only need a half hour or so. I want to check on my patients and make sure my staff doesn't feel like I abandoned them."

"I doubt they feel that way."

"You know what I mean. They need to know I'm still around and should be called with any concerns that come up." Although she had to admit the staff at the clinic were very good at their jobs. "And I want my car back. Or at least a vehicle of my own. I'll rent one for the time being."

His face stilled. "That's awfully expensive. I doubt it's in the RRPD budget."

"I'll pay for it myself."

"Of course you will."

"Wait a minute—why does that sound like an accusation?" She'd had her share of being judged because of the Colton fortune. Some people had a hard time believing a wealthy person had the same morals as the average citizen.

"You're used to being able to pay for whatever you want, I'd assume. It's a fair assessment, isn't it? Your father is Fenwick Colton. He practically owns all of South Dakota."

"Not true. He owns the most successful energy company in the state, yes." Colton Energy was having some financial issues, but Patience knew her dad would find a way to regroup. A way that hopefully didn't include Layla marrying as part of some deal. "And do I have a trust fund? Of course—but as I've already told you, I haven't touched it except to take loans out for college and vet school. And due to scholarships and the K9 research I did, I was able to pay back into said trust fund entirely. I paid for my schooling, my town house and the cabin all on my own." She felt a niggle of guilt and blurted out its cause. "Okay, I used a little bit of the funds to renovate the cabin. It was better than accepting the huge McMansion my father wanted to give me after I graduated." She and all her siblings had offered to turn their trust funds over to Fenwick to help out the business, but he'd said all of them combined would barely make a dent in the issues.

"If I were your father and could afford it, I'd give you the world after such a great accomplishment."

"You obviously love your siblings, and I've no doubt you'd do anything for them. What am I saying? You *are* doing everything for them. You've given up a single lifestyle for them. But my father isn't as altruistic. He never supported me going to vet school. He was beyond annoyed that I refused to major in finance or business at university, like Layla did. Layla's our daddy's favorite—because she works for Colton Energy."

"I know Layla."

He said it in a neutral manner, but Patience read past his ambiguous demeanor. Everyone in town knew Layla; she was an assertive, take-no-prisoners businesswoman at Colton Energy. And unknown to Nash, she was secretly engaged to that slimy jerk Hamlin. The thought of it made Patience's stomach more queasy than the baby did.

"Tell me, if you're not close to your father, why do you still call him Daddy?"

His question caught her up short. "Habit's the easiest answer. But I guess I've never stopped being the daughter who wants her father's approval. I don't need it, and don't care about it now, but it would have been nice if just once he'd acknowledged my work, you know?" She shrugged. "Maybe it's a way to keep him smaller in my mind, to not have him be that bigger-than-life person that his reputation promotes."

"It must be hard being a Colton."

"Are you being sarcastic?"

"No, I'm serious. Everyone knows your family name, and makes immediate judgments."

"Except you. You've never given me the impression you think less, or more, of me because I'm a Colton. Except for this recent slam."

"I'm sorry, Patience." Sincerity laced his tone.

She shrugged. "It's okay. Just don't do it again." She heard the edge to her words too late. "My turn to be sorry, Nash. Knowing the Lake Killer is looking for me is affecting my attitude."

"Completely normal." He stared through the windshield and she knew he, too, felt extra stress—the stress of protecting her.

The road stretched out in front of them for the last thirty minutes of the drive.

"This is going to get old, Nash. Driving back and forth to the cabin. You and Greta need to be closer to town, in case of an emergency, don't you?"

"Not happening, Patience. And stop trying to manipulate your way out of it."

Underneath her independence she had a moment of serenity—or was it relief?—that Nash was going to keep her safe from the Lake Killer.

Sometimes it didn't hurt to have a partner.

Nash pulled into the station lot, killed the engine and turned to Patience. "Take as long as you need in there. I'll work out finding you a plain car to use for now. You're right, you need to be able to come and go as needed. But I'm only going to agree to this if you don't fight me on staying overnight with you at the cabin. You'll need at least two weapons—a rifle and your RRPD-issued .45—with you at all times and in the cabin. And if I have to remain in town past usual hours you'll have to stay near me, too. I don't want you at the cabin alone for any stretch of time."

Her face was a study in conflict as she bit her lip, her eyes bright with anger. "I'm not one of your siblings, Nash. And don't you need to get back home to them? Your aunt and uncle can't stay forever, can they?"

"Actually, they can. They both work from home and run their own business on their laptops. And this won't take forever. We'll catch the man you saw on the lake, Patience."

"Let's go." She let herself out of the car and walked up to the station.

Nash stayed in his seat for a minute. "We've got to give her space, Greta. But we're not backing down on the baby business." He spoke to the dog as he watched Patience go into the building, then turned and looked at his K9 partner. "We're going to have another member of the family. Two, if she'll ever agree to raise the baby with me."

"Pale blue eyes with a vacant look to them." Patience gave the sketch artist every single detail she remembered. She'd seen that kind of expression only once before, when she'd had to testify in court against a hardened drug dealer who'd shot at one of the K9s. Patience had saved the dog's life, since local police officers had brought the injured Malinois to her within minutes, a tourniquet around its left hind leg.

"Are you sure you saw the color in the dark?" The sketch artist kept moving her hand as she questioned Patience.

"Like I said, the moon was full and I was using binoculars. I'd gone out to see if the great horned owls were in their usual perch and instead saw this man dumping a body."

"You said he had short hair?"

"Yes. That was harder to tell, as he was wearing a dark ski cap, but I noticed blond or gray hair coming out around it." Her hands started shaking and the artist noted the fact.

"Take a sip of water. We can break at any time."

"I'm okay. I know you'll get a better likeness the more I remember, and that memory fades quickly." She hadn't expected it to be so tough, but the Lake Killer wanted her dead. Of course, it would be scary going over his appearance again.

"We've got a lot already. How does this look?" The

artist turned her smart tablet around and revealed what she had so far.

Patience gasped. "I had no idea you'd make it so perfect. Your talent is amazing. It's like you took a photograph of him!"

The woman smiled. "It's my job. Lucky for us, your observational skills are top-notch. Sometimes I barely get more than the description of eyes and a nose out of a witness, trust me."

"So we're done?"

She nodded. "For now. I'll get this uploaded to our system."

Patience thanked the artist and went in search of Nash. He was in a meeting with the chief and other officers, but saw her as she passed by the conference area, and waved her over. He motioned for her to take the empty chair next to his.

"Any luck?" he whispered, leaning close to her ear. The intimate contact of his heated breath on her skin made her self-conscious, but not before her body reacted. The warmth only Nash lit fired in her belly and reached out to her most intimate parts. She looked around, but the other officers paid scant notice to her as they listened to Finn, who was outlining the details of the case so far.

"Yes," she whispered back, then saw the image of the criminal flash up on the RRPD smart board. "It's there!"

Nash turned to look and Finn nodded at Patience.

"Thank you, Dr. Colton." He used her formal title in front of the others. "You've provided a detailed description to our artist. This is the man we're looking for, everyone."

"Chief, is there any chance this is also the Groom Killer?" One of the officers spoke up and Patience stiffened. The Groom Killer was why so many in town, including Layla, had canceled long-planned weddings and postponed announcing their engagements.

"Doubtful. We've just got information that the victim was wrapped up in drug dealing. We'll know more as soon as the coroner releases his report, but I think we're looking at a different case. But we're not sure about anything until proven, right?"

"When are we going to sweep the lake again?" Nash asked, and the chief called up the officer in charge of the lake crime scene.

"I'll let Officer Billings fill you in."

Tom Billings nodded. "Good afternoon, everyone. As the chief said, we've done an initial sweep and found no further bodies, but we're going to need to dive to figure out what our equipment was catching on. It could be a sunken boat, but we're not sure. Nash, I'll need you and Greta in the morning at first light."

"You got it."

Patience leaned close to Nash. "I need to go to the clinic now, and then I'll come back with you in the morning."

She heard his sharp intake of breath, saw the pulse pounding on the side of his temple. He didn't want to leave her side and she didn't want to lose the sense of connection to him. But they were both professionals and had a job to do. Whatever it would take to catch both killers.

Patience, like Nash, prided herself on putting duty first. But her vocation didn't keep her from wishing things were different. That she and Nash could spend time together, at her cabin, for reasons other than security.

Nash drove Patience to the K9 facility. Leaving her there dismayed him, but it was still light out and she wouldn't be alone for long. He procured her a car from the station pool, an old beat-up sedan that looked nothing like the late-model SUV she normally drove. That vehicle would stay parked in the RRPD lot, so if the murderer knew it was her car, he wouldn't follow her to the cabin.

"Here are my keys." She opened a desk drawer in her office and handed him her key ring. "It's touchless."

"I think I can figure it out."

"I didn't mean to insinuate you couldn't."

They looked at one another for a heartbeat.

"Is it always going to be this prickly between us?" He knew she didn't feel her best, being newly pregnant, but thought maybe he'd done something to tick her off.

She exhaled forcefully and it made the wisps of hair around her face float. "I'm sorry, Nash. It's been a little intense, hasn't it? I mean, I know we're both in the business of adrenaline rushes, you more so than I. But I'm used to having downtime each day after surgery, and the other day was insane. We had an emergency gunshot wound and…"

"And?"

She let her shoulders fall and leaned against the wall behind her desk. "And nothing. It sounds so tame after witnessing a murderer dump a body into a lake."

"Don't forget being chased and then stalked by the killer." He knew she'd already compartmentalized what had happened. It was the only way she'd be able to walk in here again and not curl up into a protective ball on her worn office sofa.

"Yeah, well, there's that, too. But none of this is really out of the ordinary for you and Greta, is it? Not that you see murderers every day, but you're more used to the break-ins and chasing vandals. Am I right?"

"You are. But there's nothing like the stress of an op that turns personal. This case was personal for you the minute you identified the man dumping the body. Speaking of which, I have more news."

"Oh?"

"Turns out it was a young student from the community college in Rapid City. Her name was Dallas Remington, and she was nineteen and suspected of dealing heroin."

"If she was in school in Rapid City, what was she doing way up here?" Rapid City was almost two hours away in the southwest portion of the state, mirror opposite to Red Ridge's location.

"Probably picking up a drug delivery. We've had a lot of heroin activity recently and this ties in with it."

"What a shame." Patience studied him and Nash had to admit he didn't mind it when her attention was on him. "You must worry about your siblings. The opioid epidemic is alarming."

He nodded. "I sure as hell do. Being a police officer never protects a family from crime, even though I wish it did. But it's frustrating to know so much about what it can do to a kid and not be able to do anything but educate."

"And some hope and prayers, too, I imagine." She had a soft smile that he remembered from after they'd made love the first time in the middle of the night. "You can't do it all, Nash."

"No one's asking me to. I do the best I can." He needed to get back to the station. "Text me when you leave here, and when you're safe in the cabin. Take your weapon with you, and make sure it's loaded. And please, above all else, don't hesitate to use it if you need to."

"Do you really think I'd think twice if I see that monster again?"

She had him there.

Chapter 9

The next morning, they rose before sunup, and Patience beat him to the kitchen. When he walked in from his shower, the coffee was hot and she was at the stove.

"Good morning. I'm making some eggs—want one?"

"Sure, I'll take three if you have them."

She laughed. "Scrambled okay?"

"Perfect." He watched her out of the corner of his eye as he poured himself coffee. "You don't seem to be having morning sickness."

"Oh, trust me, I do, but it hits me at the oddest times. And I woke up craving eggs, so I'm not going to argue. My guess is that I need the protein."

"My guess is that you're exhausted from all we've been through, plus making a baby while you're at it."

He wasn't sure what he felt, standing in Patience's

kitchen at five thirty in the morning, but it wasn't unpleasant. A warmth pervaded the atmosphere and even Greta was perkier than usual. He nodded at her as she sat near the counter stools. "She bother you?"

"Not at all. I took her out for a quick walk while you were in the shower."

"You didn't have to. She would have waited for me."

"I figured as much, but she knows me and I knew you'd trust me with her." And she was correct—he'd trust his life with Patience, and certainly his K9.

"You know all of the RRPD dogs better than anyone, except for their handlers."

"That's my job." She served the fluffy eggs up on an aqua plate. "Here you go. And don't get used to it. I'm usually a quick yogurt or smoothie girl in the mornings."

"This looks delicious." He sat at the high counter and dug in. Between bites, he tried not to stare at her. Patience Colton first thing in the morning was a beautiful sight. "Thank you."

"You're welcome. Was the sofa comfortable? I see you gave in and used the pullout."

"I did. Greta is settling in, keeping guard at the front door. I have to say I never heard anything strange or out of place. Besides, Greta would have alerted if anyone tried to snoop around."

"Not happening. We've taken good precautions with the cars, and trust me, I made sure this place was off the map enough when I bought it. I needed a respite."

"Normally I wouldn't agree with you. Someone who's determined enough will always find who they're looking for. But this is very remote, even though I noticed you didn't say 'off the grid.'" He couldn't keep the grin off his face. Patience liked her creature comforts and Wi-Fi was included.

"No, I'm definitely not a doomsdayer! And as you noticed yesterday, I am a bit of a technophile."

"What's attractive about you, Patience, is that you don't have to have all the best, all the time. You'd never have taken the K9 position, or even be a vet, if you weren't able to put the needs of others above yours." The K9 clinic was practically brand-new and a sparkling facility, but it was still a vet's clinic. Her office sofa had already become worn in a short time from all the dogs she allowed on it.

"Thank you. No one's ever said that to me before." She sat next to him with her own plate of eggs. "I'm used to folks just assuming I'm a spoiled Colton. At least when I was younger. Now they take me for who I am, more or less."

Nash wanted to take her in every way imaginable. But that was a conversation he suspected wouldn't go over too well. Patience had made it clear that there was no hope for a relationship, or at least a repeat or two of their spectacular night together. Yesterday had been an anomaly.

He had no choice but to respect her wishes on that, but he wasn't going to give up on being a full parent for the baby. The question was how could he get past Patience's strength and independence to show her it was okay to lean on him for the baby's sake?

* * *

By the time Nash and Greta were at the dive scene, the lake was spotted with local fishing vessels, but not nearly as many as during the warmer seasons. Fall was wrapping up in Red Ridge and the morning chill proved it. In his dive suit and scuba gear, Nash wasn't looking forward to the water temperature.

"Greta, stay." Nash and Greta were on a police patrol boat with four other officers, anchored over the sight where the victim had been found. The RRPD and a local coast guard unit had guarded the area since the night of the murder. A basic drag of the lake hadn't revealed any more bodies, but a couple sonar hits in this area had alerted the RRPD that there might be something still hiding in the lake.

Greta let out two sharp barks, her signal that something was going on below the water. RRPD Officer Cathy Schwab was working the bottom of the lake, and Nash was up next.

"Has Cathy found anything yet?" Nash spoke to Tom Billings, the officer in charge.

"Yes, but I couldn't make out what. She's coming up now." Tom looked overboard to where the diver's figure was visible as she rose from the lake's bottom. He held his headset tight to his ear.

"It could be why Greta is alerting, but we'll be on the lookout for anything off." Nash spoke to the team as much as to himself. He trusted Greta's instincts and didn't believe she'd alert over Cathy's movements.

"Nash, you ready?" Tom spoke as he checked Nash's oxygen tanks while they waited for her to surface.

Within seconds she was alongside the boat and the two other officers hauled her back on board.

Officer Schwab stripped off her hood and mask as the dive team worked to untether her safety line and attach it to Nash's harness. "There's definitely something there, and it looked like a fluorescent orange flag marks the spot. But I had to surface—I was out of air and feeling hypothermic. I felt cold almost right away, Nash. Don't expect to stay down for too long."

"We need heated wet suits." Nash knew he'd stay as long as he could in the icy water, but the department rule was safety first.

"Funding is everything. Why don't you ask Dr. Colton while you're hanging with her? She can get her father to throw us some support." Tom referred to the fact that Fenwick Colton had almost single-handedly donated the funds to pay for the new upgrades at the K9 training center, making the decades-old building practically brand-new, with a full extension and indoor training pool. It was where the team practiced this kind of dive.

"I'll get right on that." Nash's reply made the entire team laugh. "I'm going in. What do I have, ten minutes?" He looked at Cathy.

She nodded. "It's the most you can hope for in these temperatures."

Nash put on his mask, made sure the underwater breathing apparatus was working and gave Tom a thumbs-up.

He plunged into the water. As much as he'd braced for the shock of the cold, nothing ever prepared him for it. Grateful for his wet suit, he got to work. The lamp on his headgear lit up the surrounding area, clearer than usual. The cold temperature affected the sediment and dirt twenty feet below the surface, too. Still, he waited for a light cloud of dirt and sand to settle. Once it did, he focused on the area Cathy had directed him to, and within seconds saw the flag she'd been talking about.

"Eyes on flag. Going there now." He had to modulate his breathing in order to talk. He kept communication to a minimum when he dived.

Nash swam to the flag, a triangular orange cloth attached to a long white flexible pole. He found two sealed containers at the base of it, nestled against a large boulder, and reached down to see if he could lift them. They were light enough, and upon further inspection, he saw they were waterproof ones used by divers and fishermen.

"Nash, abort mission and surface now. Repeat, abort mission." Tom's voice sounded in his earpiece.

He felt a sharp tug on his safety line, another emergency signal that demanded he surface immediately.

"Why, Tom?" he asked over the comm unit. He had seven minutes left on his watch. But there was no reply from Tom, not even a rush of static. As dive master, Tom's orders were sacrosanct. Nash grabbed one of the boxes and prepared to surface.

Before he could, the large form of Greta appeared, swimming straight for him. Why had Tom deployed Greta while ordering Nash to surface? He signaled for her to surface, too.

Greta either didn't see his hand signals or ignored

him, completely unlike her. As she swam not to him, but past him, Nash turned. Adrenaline surged when he saw her target—another diver, male, who was not RRPD. The man held a knife in his hand and Nash realized that must have been the tug he'd felt—his line had been cut. That same knife meant trouble for Greta.

Greta had the other diver's arm in her teeth and was making for the surface with him when he saw the man strike her head with his free hand. Nash feared she'd been stabbed and knew Greta needed air, so he signaled her to surface while he went after the assailant.

The thug knocked the container from Nash's grip and grabbed the second one, wielding his knife in a clear message: he'd kill Nash for the boxes. Nash didn't have body armor on, and even if he had, it wasn't bladeproof. He was a strong swimmer and diver, even with the weight vest. But he found himself struggling to breathe, and at the same time, his tank issued a loud warning alarm. The thug had cut his air off, too. He had no choice but to surface. And pray that Greta was okay.

Patience stood on the edge of the lake, watching as the RRPD launch approached the small dock. It was all she could do not to jump into the water to reach Nash sooner, to hell with the cold. If not for their unborn child, she would. When she'd heard the alert over the clinic's sound system she'd had to fight off the urge to throw up. Greta was injured, and that meant Nash had been in harm's way.

As the boat cut across the usually placid lake, sadness hit her that what had been her secret serenity spot had turned deadly overnight. Literally.

Greta wagged her tail as the boat neared, even though her head was held by Nash, keeping her still. Thank God, Nash appeared none the worse for wear.

Patience ignored the other dive team members, focused solely on him. She made eye contact with Nash as the boat came alongside the concrete pier. It wasn't necessary for her to jump into the vessel, but she wanted to. Best to keep it professional, though, since Greta didn't appear seriously injured.

"You okay?" She wanted him to know she cared. He was still in a wet suit, but it was unzipped, his RRPD jacket and ski cap providing warmth.

"I'm good. Greta got stabbed." He held the dog's head in his lap, pressing a gauze bandage to it. The red stain that spread on the white fabric told her he was keeping it under control, but she suspected Greta was going to need stitches at the very least.

Greta looked up at her with soulful eyes and Patience smiled. "You're going to be just fine, girl." She returned her attention to Nash and the dive team. "Did anyone see what happened to her?"

"I did." Nash stood and helped Greta get off the boat. Patience pointed for her to lie down on the lowered stretcher, which Greta did with her bulky frame as gracefully as any sugarplum fairy in *The Nutcracker*. Patience buckled the dog onto the cot before she stood and pressed the button to raise the stretcher to working height. Nash went to push Greta but Patience put her hand on his arm. "They've got her."

Two vet techs expertly moved Greta up the pier and onto the ramp at the back of the clinic.

"I think she's fine. It looks like she just got a cut on her scruff. An unknown diver attacked me and her. They made off with containers we discovered. A patrol was dispatched to intercept the diver but they've found nothing." Nash issued the report with professional expertise, but she saw his pallor, the pulse at his temple throbbing under his skin. He'd obviously been through an event, and with the cold conditions could go into shock. He needed to warm up.

"I've got her, Nash. Go get a hot shower and find us when you're dressed."

She didn't wait for him to respond, but instead ran to Greta's side. All the K9s were vital to the RRPD's work and she treated them all as if they were her own. But now Greta had achieved a new status with her—she was her baby daddy's K9. Patience knew the pain it caused Nash to have his partner hurting in any way.

She walked behind Greta's gurney to the clinic. She couldn't pinpoint when or where it had happened, but Nash's well-being was inexplicably important to her. It wasn't just because of the baby, though that was the easiest explanation for the fear that had rocked her when she'd heard the alarm call for Nash and Greta.

She quickly glanced around the clinic and to its farthest visible bounds, quelling her anxiety over the Lake Killer. He was nowhere in sight. For now.

Patience quickly ascertained that Greta's cut was superficial. As she cleaned the small wound, she wondered how Nash had checked out with the EMTs the RRPD called in. If he had to go to the ER, she'd be the one to get him to the cabin tonight.

She and Greta walked to her office, where Greta settled down and Patience checked her emails.

"Nice headgear, Greta." Nash's voice made her stomach flip as he walked into her office and spoke to his K9, who'd taken up her favorite spot on the largest of three dog beds. Often Patience would have one of the dogs stay with her after it had been through either a daily drill with its partner or the monthly group training session. Patience knew the K9s needed to accept her as worthy of trust, so that they'd allow her to treat them in a worst-case scenario. Which, unfortunately, she'd done on several occasions.

"Greta's doing fine." She pushed back from the side of her desk, where she'd been working on the computer. "You were right. It was a very minor cut. And while I know the knife wound scared you, it was a clean cut and I didn't even have to stitch it."

"You were able to glue it?"

She nodded. "She's absolutely fine. But no diving until it's healed, of course. I'd give it a week, at least. We don't want to risk infection. Because it's on the top of her scruff she can't get to it, so I'll send her home without a cone. How does she usually do when she's hurt?"

"She only needed a cone after she was spayed." Nash was on his haunches next to his dog. "You did a good job today, Greta."

Greta's huge tail thumped against the floor and they both laughed.

"She's a special dog. What happened out there, Nash?" Patience was worried there might be more victims. She was haunted by it since the other night.

"No more bodies, if that's what you're asking." Nash's direct answer was predictable, but she still felt as though he could read her mind. And if that in turn meant he was able to read her heart, it spelled trouble. As she watched him love on Greta, she felt a tug under her rib cage, suspiciously near her heart. Baby daddy or not, Nash was a man she could fall for. If she'd lost him today…

"How did she get cut, Nash?" Staying in the present always proved handy for keeping the what-ifs at bay.

He stood up and walked closer to her. "There was another diver there, an unknown. Good chance it was the same guy who tried to come after you both times, but no way of telling with all the dive equipment on both of us. I couldn't see the color of his eyes. He cut my lifeline and messed up my tanks. I couldn't go after him, but between the other dive officer and me, the dive team was able to verify that it was a spot used to exchange drugs or money. Or both. I saw him swim off with two plastic containers before I had to surface."

His frustration was palpable in the small space between them. The clinic beyond her office was bustling as routine appointments were handled and techs walked dogs to and from the back fenced area and training yard.

"You're lucky you're still here, Nash." She didn't have to tell him it'd been a close call. And she didn't want to tell him how much it had shaken her. He'd been her rock over the past two days.

"If I'd seen him first, we'd have the contraband, if that's what it is. And he'd be in cuffs." His gaze never faltered. "If something had happened to me, what would you have done? I mean, about the baby?"

She saw the question in his eyes, deeper than the one he verbalized. He wondered if she had been worried about him.

"I'm glad you're okay, if that's what you're asking. If the worst happened—and it didn't—nothing would be different. I would raise the baby like I'm going to. On my own." She took a step back, but her calves hit her chair and she wobbled. When he grasped her upper arms and steadied her she felt the connection to her very center. A whoosh of air left her lungs and the tension left her body. Nash was okay. He'd survived.

"Are you sure about that, Patience? Why are you still so bent on your independence?" His hazel eyes glittered. It reminded her of the night they'd spent together, of how intensely intimate it had been.

"Of—of course I'm sure. You say 'independence' like it's a bad thing." She couldn't help licking her lips as he stared at her. He looked hungry. Starving. Her body leaned closer, any resistance to her attraction to Nash futile.

"I think you're might be overlooking the obvious."

He closed the gap and his lips came down on hers with the most delicious amount of purpose. She wrapped her arms around his neck and gave the kiss, the embrace, Nash her all. It was too hard not to.

Nash loved the feel of Patience in his arms, and liked the taste of her lips even more. He nudged her lips apart with his tongue and hers was there, waiting for him. The friction of their tongues after a life-threatening scenario proved as intimate as making love, and he pulled her against him, not satisfied with just mouth contact.

Patience groaned and the sheer need in her voice mirrored what he felt, as his desire for her went from a spark to combustion in two seconds flat. He wanted—no, he *needed*—her to feel what he'd experienced in the lake, under the water, too far from her. The pure terror that he might never see her again, never hold her like this. That he might never meet his unborn son or daughter.

Patience pulled back and removed her hands from around his neck, but at least she let them rest on his chest as she stared at him. A small comfort. Did she have any idea how desirable she was? Her eyes were big and dark, shining from the ardor of their embrace, and her lips were swollen. He was proud of that, that his kiss did this to her.

"What?" He bent to nuzzle behind her ear, inhaling her scent.

"Nash." Her hands were firmer this time as she pushed on his chest, just a little. "We're at work."

"So?" He watched her eyes reflect arousal, amusement, frustration. He took a step back and shook his head. Had he suffered from more oxygen deprivation than he'd initially thought? "Heck, Patience, I'm sorry. You're right. I think the dive, and how messed up it got, has me leaving my manners at the door."

"It's not your manners, Nash." She looked at her door before running her hand down his arm in a conciliatory gesture. "It's the fact that we could be seen at any point. It'd be one thing if we were, you know. A couple. I don't want anyone to get the wrong idea."

A chill ran down his back, quickly followed by a rush of heat. "Whatever."

She shook her head. "I don't mean it like that, Nash."

"Like what? Like you have absolutely no interest in getting to know me past the sex we've shared? Like you're embarrassed to be caught with me, a regular kind of guy without a trust fund?"

She blinked and swayed as if his words were physical. Remorse flooded him, but he held his ground. Patience needed to get used to him being around, because she was going to have his child and he was going to be a participatory father.

"You know I don't care how much is in your, or anyone else's, bank account." She looked away, as if it were her fault he'd snapped.

"I know you don't. I'm sorry. It's been a long day. It wasn't fun, this dive."

She nodded. "Are you okay to drive?"

"Yes. If I had any doubt, I wouldn't."

"Okay, then, I'll see you back at the cabin. Do you mind if Greta stays with me? I'd like to keep an eye on her for the rest of the day, just in case she shows any other effects of the dive."

"That's fine." He had so much to catch up on at the station, and he wanted to be home when the kids got off school. His aunt and uncle were doing a great job, no doubt, but he didn't want any of his siblings to think that he'd abandoned them. "I've got to stop in and see the kids."

"Of course you do. Normally I would insist you go back home, but I have to admit I'm worried, Nash. I keep thinking the Lake Killer is behind the next corner. Since I can't go to your place, as the kids' safety comes first, you need to do so. And take whatever time you need to."

"I didn't peg you as the maternal type." Of course, he'd only ever interacted with her in the clinic during training and Greta's exams, before their physical relationship began.

"You don't seem like the fatherly type, either, but you're doing it." She tilted her head. "We don't know one another very well at all, do we?"

"Oh, I'd say we know one another *very* well." He winked at her and enjoyed watching the blush color her cheeks. Patience Colton was worldly and sophisticated, yet still humble and very flirt-worthy. "Seriously, I do feel like I've known you longer than I have." Yet she spoke the truth: they needed to know one another better.

"We've worked together a long while—what, at least the past three years, since I got out of vet school, right?"

"Something like that." He remembered hearing that she'd been a prodigy of sorts and completed college and vet school earlier than most. But there wasn't time to talk about it now. They both had work to do.

"I'll see you later." He knelt and scratched Greta under her chin, to avoid disturbing her cut. "You be good for Patience."

"See you back h—at the cabin." Patience almost said *home*. She watched him, something alight in her eyes that he didn't want to explore.

He left her office and told himself the pang deep in his chest had to be from Greta getting hurt this morning. It wasn't as if he couldn't live without Patience Colton.

Chapter 10

Patience sat in the booth at the front window of the restaurant. As she watched her older sister walk into their
favorite Red Ridge café she couldn't keep the smile
from her face. Nash would be angry if he knew she'd
sneaked out of the clinic to meet Layla for a late lunch,
but Patience had taken precautions by wearing a bulky
hooded jacket and driving an RRPD civilian vehicle.
She hadn't noticed anyone following her, and felt rea-
sonably safe in the local restaurant.

She waved Layla over from the hostess's desk.

Patience's only full sibling, Bea, was as eager as their
father for the Groom Killer to be caught, as it was eating into her bridal business, too. But Bea, compassionate and kind, was nothing like Fenwick. Patience spent
time with Bea as she was able, but Bea had never been

the sister she'd bonded the most closely with. Layla had. She saw Blake often enough, as Juliette was an RRPD K9 officer, and their youngest sister, Gemma, came around to the clinic every now and then as she spent her time fund-raising for animal causes. But neither Bea nor Gemma knew her like Layla did.

Patience thought she and Layla had bonded because they'd both inherited the Colton drive. Layla, as VP of Colton Energy, directed her strengths to the family business, while Patience threw herself into the K9 clinic. Patience had never had an interest in business at all but from a career standpoint understood Layla's need to succeed.

They were so different people often forgot they were sisters, even with the same last name. Layla was polished from head to toe. Her blond bob was sleek as ever today and contrasted sharply with her ice-blue power suit that matched her eyes. She had never given a nod to living in a more rural area by adopting comfortable shoes or cowboy boots, and was wearing her classic black designer stilettos. Sometimes Patience wondered if Layla hid her sweet nature behind her corporate look. Layla was determined to keep the family business going no matter what.

"Hey, sis." Layla kissed Patience on the cheek before she eased into the booth after grabbing a napkin and wiping the seat off. She grinned at Patience. "It's wonderful to see you. How are you doing?"

Patience froze. *The baby.* Would Layla see it? Notice her big belly?

"I'm great. I missed you."

"I've missed you, too. Let's order so that we can talk." Layla opened her menu, but then craned her head toward the large blackboard behind the coffee bar. "What are today's specials?"

"Pan-fried trout, an endive-and-citrus salad and their carrot cake."

Layla turned to face her. "Split a slice with me?"

"You know it."

The waitress delivered ice water and asked for their orders. Patience wasn't sure about fish with the baby, so she stuck to a plain grilled cheese, while Layla went for the endive salad.

"We're going to split a piece of the carrot cake later." Layla handed her menu to the waitress, as did Patience.

Once the server was out of earshot, Patience spoke. "It's okay to wait to order dessert. Are you afraid it'll disappear before we get to eat it?" She couldn't help poking at Layla. It was what they did—criticizing one another so that no one else could surprise them with their slams. It was an old habit from when they were kids and bullied for being so wealthy. They'd never told their father or mothers about it because they'd begged to go to the public school and had all their friends there. But they also had a few enemies.

"You know my sweet tooth. And why aren't you drinking your usual diet soda?"

Darn Layla and her sharp power of observation.

"I thought I'd try to be healthier. Besides, the caffeine's been bothering my sleep."

"Really?" Layla's perfectly made-up face was breathtaking in its beauty and Patience wondered for the millionth time why her sister would agree to marry Hamlin Harrington just to save Colton Energy. How could she sign away her own happiness that way?

"Hmm." She was not going there with Layla. Not today.

"You look like you're disappointed in me again, Patience. Please tell me we're not going to rehash the Hamlin issue."

"I have no intention of that. Not at all. But really, Layla, you just called your own fiancé an 'issue.' You can't tell me you're in love with the man."

"Some things are more important than personal happiness. Like family and legacy." Layla's resignation saddened Patience.

"Layla, please know I only want what's best for you. You deserve to be happy. When it's the right person, it's not a sacrifice."

Layla flashed her a surprised glance. Shoot. She'd meant what she'd said, more proof that she was getting in deep with Nash. Too deep.

"Wait, what? You're dating someone, aren't you?" Layla leaned over the table, her pearls glistening as the midday sun shone through the café's front window.

Patience held her eye contact without flinching. "No. Absolutely not."

"Come on, Patience. Spill it."

"There's nothing to spill. I'm single, unattached." Liar. At least where the baby was concerned.

Layla kept giving her the look that only a sister can. The "I'm going to sit here and wait until you dish" look.

Patience groaned. "You have to promise not to tell

Daddy." No matter how angry she or Layla got at their often absent father, they still referred to him with their childhood label.

"Cross my heart. As long as you stop harassing me over Hamlin."

"Deal. But you can't tell Bea, Blake or Gemma, either. I mean it." Patience took a sip of water. It was the most fortifying beverage of choice, since caffeine and alcohol were off-limits. "I'm pregnant."

Layla's expression didn't change. She blinked once, twice. "Shut. The. Front. Door."

Patience nodded, and before she knew they were threatening, tears spilled down her cheeks. "I wasn't planning it, of course. In fact, we used precautions."

Layla squealed with delight and got up to come around the table and give Patience a warm hug. "Congratulations! This is very exciting." She sat back down and took a drink of water.

"I'm glad you're happy about it."

"Cut to the chase. Who's your baby daddy?" Layla at least had the sense to keep her voice low and limited to their booth. Patience looked around the full café. Most of the customers were strangers or distant acquaintances. No threat of anyone they knew overhearing, anyway.

"I don't want to reveal that yet."

"Is he going to step up to the plate and help you with the baby?"

"Why do you assume I want or need help raising a child?"

"It's me, Patience. Your loving sister. We're Coltons.

We like to have children. It's the raising them right that we struggle with. All I'm saying is that it might not be a bad idea for you to have the other parent there alongside you to balance your quirks."

Patience laughed. "That's not an understatement." Fenwick had always meant well, but he'd been an absent father at best, always putting work first. "Daddy's still a business-first guy, but he has seemed happier lately, when we're all together."

"What, at Christmas after a few single-malt scotches?" Layla shrugged. "We're a modern family. It's a miracle we all get under one roof together to celebrate anything these days."

The waitress brought their food and they paused until she walked away.

"Have you heard anything on the Groom Killer?" Layla spoke as she smoothed three paper napkins over her lap and suit front.

Patience laughed. "I'm amused at how you treat that suit. And admit it—you're excited about being an auntie." She didn't want to talk about any killer during her time with Layla.

"Yes, once the shock wears off, I will pester you for a list of what you'd like for the baby. So, no news on the case?"

"No, nothing new, but you should know I'm going to be living at my cabin for the foreseeable future." She explained what had happened. Layla's eyes widened when Patience said "Lake Killer" and she put down her fork.

"You could have been killed, Patience! You have to come stay with me." Layla shuddered. "It can't be fun having a stranger, even a cop, stay with you day in and day out."

"Are you kidding? Did you hear what I said? I can't stay at Nash Maddox's because he's got four young siblings at home. We can't risk the killer following me there. No way do I want you in danger, either." She personally felt Layla had enough on her hands with her slimy fiancé, but kept the thought to herself. "Besides, it's part of my job description, even if it's unusual. I know the RRPD K9s and their handlers as well as I know my family. We're a team and we help each other."

Layla sighed. "I wish I had that. The work-is-a-family thing. You know I love my job and the challenges it brings, but I can't say there's a lot of camaraderie at Colton Energy."

"It's all about pleasing one man, that's why. Fenwick Colton. And you and he are working together all the time, with just your staff to support you. I work for the community when it comes down to it. The RRPD and the K9 teams all serve the public. We have to work together, no matter the personalities."

"Are you going to be able to work there after the baby comes?"

"Of course. I'll need to find childcare, of course, but nothing more than any other working woman faces. And I make a good living." She thought about her vet techs and some of the RRPD support staff. They often struggled to make ends meet, and affordable day care was often an issue.

"You don't have to work, Patience. You could take a leave of absence. In fact, maybe you should do it now.

You can disappear for a while, go abroad until they catch the man you saw on the lake. Did you tell Daddy about all of this?"

"No, not yet. I don't want him, or you, thinking that the clinic is more of a liability than an asset."

Layla stared at her. "Even I know it's not a business asset. Red Ridge needs your clinic, and I'll do my best to keep the funding on track. It's not about that, anyhow. It's your mother's legacy to the community."

"You won't be able to do anything if Daddy says to shut it down."

"There are other sources of funding if he does, but he won't. He has his hands full right now."

"Like trying to make sure he keeps Hamlin on his side and supporting Colton Energy?"

Layla's gaze sharpened. "We are going to have to agree to disagree on my choice of future husband. Hamlin can save Colton Energy."

"I'm sure Daddy can find another way, Layla. You can't tell me there's a lot of chemistry between you two!"

"Sex isn't everything."

Patience tried not to frown. She loved Layla and wanted her to be happy, not chained to a false sense of duty.

A movement outside caught her eye and she noted a tall woman walking two dogs. Two very familiar dogs. Her pulse quickened. She would know the adult Belgian Malinois, Nico, anywhere. She'd helped when his mother had whelped him and his littermates, and done a lot of the initial training, which was continued by Danica Gage, one of the Red Ridge K9 center's dog trainers. Patience was certain the slightly smaller dog next to him was definitely the Malinois pup that had been stolen along with Nico, back in May. The puppy would be that exact size by now.

"I'm sorry, but I've got to go, Layla." She stood up, ready to break for the door.

"I do, too. Wait—are you okay, Patience?"

"Yes. I'll call you later, promise. Pay the check, will you? Next time's on me!" She ran from the café, ignoring the cold wind that whipped down Main Street.

Lucky for her, the dogs weren't with the dangerous Larson brothers, who Patience and Danica believed had been behind the theft. And the dog walker had been stupid enough to leave the dogs tied outside the café. The woman was nowhere to be seen, but Patience wasn't waiting for her to return. She approached Nico with confidence, but carefully, just in case he didn't remember her.

"Nico."

The dog cocked his head, his intelligent expression the same as she remembered. After a few moments she held out her hand for him to sniff, which he did, then immediately licked, adding a happy yip to the affectionate gesture. He remembered her!

"Good boy."

The younger dog followed suit, doing whatever Nico did.

"Come on, boys, I'm springing you two loose." She unwrapped their leashes and hurriedly led them to her loaner car from the RRPD. There were no safety buckles for them like she kept in her vehicle but she'd take her chances. Her hand shook as she put the key in the ignition. She couldn't risk getting caught by the woman the Larson brothers had hired to walk the dogs. Anyone associated with the criminal twins couldn't be trusted. Patience was likely to be shot if they caught her. They'd long been on the RRPD's radar, but were great at covering their tracks. One day, one or both of the twins would slip up.

Once she was driving away, she let out a huge sigh, followed by a whoop. She'd gotten Nico and the puppy back for the K9 training center!

Frustration ran its familiar hand down her spine when she remembered she didn't have a hands-free phone in this car. She'd have to wait until she got back to the clinic to call the police department.

With a jolt she realized that when she thought about letting the team know she'd gotten the dogs back, she wasn't picturing Finn or any other officer, or one of her veterinary staff. The only person in her mind was Nash.

To be fair, as frightened as she was of the Lake Killer, Nash occupied the bulk of her waking thoughts.

"Where's Dr. Colton now?" Nash stood in front of the receptionist, his heart pounding. He'd driven back to the clinic within twenty minutes of arriving at his desk. When Finn walked in and told him that Patience had "found" Nico and the puppy, now five months old, he'd been elated.

It was about time the Larson twins saw their own machinations used against them. But then the chief had gone on to explain how Patience had acquired the dogs, and Nash thought his head might explode like a cartoon character's.

"She's back in the kennels, checking on her patients." The receptionist gave him an easy smile. "Did you hear she found Nico and the pup?"

The woman's exuberance tamped down some of his ire, but not enough to keep him from making a beeline for the area.

He found Patience kneeling at the lowest row of kennels, placing the Belgian Malinois puppy in its new enclosure. The dog looked like it had as a pup, but was so much larger.

Patience must have heard Nash enter because she looked up, her hand still rubbing the pup's chest. The triumph in her eyes threw ice water on his fury.

"Hey, Nash. So you heard?" She smiled and all— well, almost all—the words of anger he'd been ready to spew, accusing her of putting herself and the baby at huge risk, dissolved on his tongue.

"Son of a—" He stopped himself and knelt next to her. Peering into the crate, he saw the pup that Danica Gage had just started to work with before he was stolen. "He's so much bigger. They both check out okay?"

Patience nodded. "Yes."

"Where's Nico?" He was relieved the adult Malinois was back in the RRPD K9 family, but not that it put Patience in more danger than she already was. Noel and Evan Larson were despicable, cruel men.

"Out in the back field. Danica couldn't wait to put him through some training exercises, to reacquaint them both."

"She must be over the moon."

"Yes, for sure." Patience closed the kennel door. "Have a good nap, buddy."

"Do you think he'll settle back in here that easily?"

"We just wore him out on the agility course. He's not had any formal training since he was stolen, from what we could tell. But he's eager to learn, trusts us and will pretty much do whatever Nico does. In fact, it's fair to say that Nico saved both of their lives. He didn't fight the Larsons, but followed the training we'd already given him, which protected the pup."

"He have a name?"

"Not yet. We'll go through our usual process to name him." The RRPD's policy to name K9s involved the community. The dog's photo would be put on social media and Red Ridge citizens were asked to offer suggestions. The elementary schools were all involved, with each classroom coming up with one name to put forward. The chamber of commerce voted on the final choice.

"The Larson twins are going to have a fit when they see that." Nash stood and helped her up. "Speaking of which, the real reason I came back today wasn't to see the dogs, Patience."

"I thought maybe you were still worried about Greta."

"I was worried about *you*. You know who the Larsons are, what they're capable of. If one of them had seen you take their dog, I could have lost you both."

"Us…both?" She stared at him for what felt like forever. "I wasn't thinking about anything but getting the dogs back to where they belong. God knows what they went through with those men."

"I don't care about that. I care about you. And the baby." His insides felt as soft and warm as her eyes appeared. What was it about Patience Colton that made him forget his reason for coming here? That made him think he could willingly fall into a serious relationship with her, something more than co-parenting?

"Okay. I hear you. You're not the only one getting used to the baby, you know. I only knew about him, or her, a few hours before you did."

"I know you said you thought you missed your two periods due to stress, but you should know your cycles better. You know about period apps, right?"

Her eyes widened and her mouth lifted on one side. "Look at you, all knowledgeable about the menstrual cycle."

He refused to be embarrassed for his lack of ignorance. "I've been raising teenage girls for the last five years. They each started their cycles under my watch. Of course, I know just about everything a man can regarding periods."

Patience's smile softened and she placed her hand on his cheek. "I've underestimated you. I'm sorry."

A loud *bam* cracked through the air as the swinging door from the reception area hit the side of the kennel wall. Patience jumped and her heart froze when she identified who'd slammed it open.

Noel and Evan Larson entered the room and walked toward them with menace stamped on their faces. "I want my dogs back. Now." Noel, known to be the ring-leader, spoke as Evan glowered.

"Hold on a minute. Who let you in here?" Patience said. Nash placed his hand on his holstered weapon, letting his body language speak to the twins.

"They cleared us at reception. Don't worry, I gave them my gun for safekeeping." Noel's sarcastic smile angered Nash. The Larsons had a bad reputation and were suspected of drug dealing in Red Ridge, and had been connected to murders, including the Groom Killer's. But their alibis were solid on the murders and there wasn't enough evidence to nail them for the drug crimes—yet. But wherever trouble was, there were the Larsons.

And they'd taken two of the K9 training center's dogs. That was fact.

The Malinois puppy growled from his kennel.

"They were never your dogs, Noel. They belong to the county and to the RRPD." Patience spoke as if she dealt with hardened criminals every day.

Noel pointed an accusing finger at her. Nash wanted to snap that finger in half, but stood his ground and let Patience do the same. He completely trusted her instinct and abilities, even with a big bad bully like Noel Larson.

"You stole them from in front of the café. My dog walker saw you! They have microchips proving my ownership."

"Calm down, Noel. You're right. That's the best way to prove canine identity and ownership. Nash, will you escort Noel and Evan to Exam Room One? I'll bring the dogs."

Nash's gut tightened. He knew the Larsons weren't

that ignorant—they would have had the dogs micro-chipped by another veterinarian as soon as they'd captured the puppies. But there was no doubt that these were the two that the Larsons had stolen. How would he keep them from the thieves, from danger? And how could he stop Patience from placing herself between the dogs and a dangerous man?

Chapter 11

Patience was quaking inside, but damned if she'd let the Larson brothers see it. The jerks had kidnapped these precious dogs and tried to pass them off as their own. Worse, they'd paraded them around town as if there were no repercussions for stealing dogs. When, in fact, they'd stolen police property.

She was beyond grateful that Nash let her take the lead and didn't challenge the Larsons or kick them out of the clinic. It would have totally been within his purview to do so, since they were acting in a threatening manner, and doing so on county government property. And with the suspected illicit drug connection between the victim she'd seen dumped into the lake and the Larsons, Nash must want to see Noel and Evan behind bars. But to his credit, he stayed cool, while shooting her reassuring glances.

He believed in her.

As if she were a foot taller and a hundred pounds heavier, she entered the exam room with Nico and the younger dog on leashes. Nash stood near the door, while Noel Larson's hulking frame was braced in the center of the room, next to the exam table. Evan leaned against the wall.

"This won't take long." She took the scanning gun from a counter drawer and turned it on. "We agree that whatever this reveals, we're all good with it, right?"

Noel met her gaze and she saw fury, indignation and the promise of revenge in his eyes. He really thought he was going to walk out of here with the dogs he'd stolen, after having one of their best K9 handlers knocked out? The memory of Danica's pain and suffering made Patience see red.

"Right, Noel? Evan?" She used all her willpower to keep from snarling at them.

"Right," Noel grunted. Evan refused to speak. Their reluctance would have been laughable if they weren't such vile men.

"Nico." She gave the hand signal for him to stand in front of her, and when he complied, she waved the wand over the space between his shoulder blades. A digital readout reflected a unique ID. She held the display up for the Larsons to see.

"This is a code assigned only to our K9 clinic."

"That's impossible! I had microchips put in those dogs the minute I got them!"

Yes, Patience thought. *Right after you stole them from*

us. As Noel complained, Evan pushed back from the wall and stood alongside his brother.

She sensed more than saw Nash close the short distance and step between her and the men.

"Tamp it down, Larson." Nash's deep baritone was smooth and professional, but to Patience, it was the definition of pure security. Nash had her back, and she and the dogs were safe.

Noel took a half step back, clearly struggling with his temper. "Wave that wand of yours over his entire body. You'll find my microchip."

"I'm happy to do that, but it doesn't matter if another microchip shows up or not. K9 property takes priority unless there's a legal contract giving ownership to a civilian. You're a civilian and there is most definitely no contract between the RRPD, the RRPD K9 training center or Red Ridge County and you. These are not your dogs, Noel." She stared at him, refusing to budge.

Noel Larson wasn't the first person she'd had to take dogs from, but in past cases it'd been because the owners had neglected or abused their animals. Noel had taken care of these dogs well enough—they'd been fed—but he'd held stolen the canines. They weren't his.

He glared at her. "I get what's mine, Doc. Don't forget it." He turned to Nash. "And you—you have nothing on me or my brother. Screw you." With that, he and Evan left the exam room.

She turned to Nash. "There's so much I wanted to say to him, but didn't. I deactivated their microchips from the Larsons, by the way, when I put in ours. I called the manufacturer and reported the Larsons' identification as illegal. It's official—they are RRPD K9 property again. As they always were."

Nash gently turned her around.

"Thank God you thought so quickly. Let me do this for you." His warm hands settled on her shoulders, massaging her tension away.

"Why are there such awful people in the world?"

"Who knows? What matters is that you handled them perfectly. Trust me, given enough time and more evidence, those two are going to end up in jail, if I or my fellow cops have anything to do with it."

"I know." She did know, and more, she trusted Nash. She turned around and gave him a quick kiss on the lips. "And I know I'm contradicting my edict to be professional, but you know what? I don't care. Noel scared the crap out of me."

"You were incredible with him." Nash's eyes shone with intensity. "You know your stuff, Dr. Colton."

She laughed. "When it comes to the animals and especially K9s? I hope I do. It's my job!"

"I'm going to make sure he's off the property. Promise me won't put yourself on the line again today? I'd like to meet you safe and sound at the cabin."

"I'll be there when you get there."

He gave her a firm kiss goodbye. Patience wished it could last longer. The only time she didn't think about the Lake Killer was when she was in Nash's arms.

Nash didn't get to see the kids until much later. He was relieved that he'd been at the clinic when the Larson twins had shown up. If his hackles weren't already up from the Lake Killer case, the Larsons would do it. The twins were bad guys and at heart, bullies. He made a mental note to ask Patience if there was any way they might know about her cabin.

He'd taken a circuitous route home, practicing evading techniques he'd learned at the police academy. He couldn't risk the Lake Killer showing up and following him. Threatening the kids. He'd missed them, for sure, but to his surprise he'd been so completely absorbed with the case he hadn't spent a lot of time thinking about them. Knowing his aunt and uncle had them helped.

You don't think about anything but Patience when you're with her.

He took a minute as he got out of his car in the driveway. Sure, he thought about Patience a lot, but wasn't that normal? She was carrying his baby!

"Nash!" Troy jogged down the driveway toward him, all limbs and squeaky voice at twelve years old. "I didn't know you were coming home." He stood awkwardly in front of Nash at an age where he wasn't sure how to show affection.

Nash immediately enveloped him in a bear hug, kissing the top of his head. "Hey, bud! I had some time and wanted to make sure you hadn't tied up Uncle Jim and Aunt Clara. You behaving?"

"Yeah." Troy shrugged out of the hug, but his grin split his face. "Paige and Maeve are keeping things going, but Maeve thinks she knows it all."

Nash laughed. His younger half sister had recently scored perfectly on the PSATs and was obsessed with the naval academy and all things military. She also had a very strong maternal instinct, which she practiced on the boys.

"What about Paige?"

"She's always at swim practice or studying." Paige, a senior, had two athletic scholarships and was hoping for more by spring semester. Nash was proud of his sister and overjoyed that something was going so right for them. Losing their parents in such a tragic manner five years ago had cast a long sad shadow over their teen years. But they'd pulled out of it, thank God.

"How's school going for you?" Nash was careful to not specifically ask about the bullies Troy had been plagued with. While he was at the top of his class academically, his brother had yet to find his place in any sport, music group or other extracurricular activity. But he was clear about wanting to go to college, at least. He'd shown an interest in marching band, and Nash planned to support him in joining it when he was eligible at the end of eighth grade. But as a seventh grader, Troy was in the thick of middle school growing pains.

"It's fine. We got to use the Bunsen burners in science lab today."

"That's fun." Nash put his arm around his brother as they walked into the house.

Maeve was predictably at the family calendar, adding the *washi* tape she was fond of to the next week.

"Hey, Maeve."

"Hi, Nash!" She gave him a quick hug before turning back to the monthly schedule. "I just filled in the activities for next week for Aunt Clara and Uncle Jim. I thought you'd still be gone."

"I probably will be. I'm working a tough case and I can't take time away until we solve it."

Maeve's eyes lit up. "Is it about the Lake Dumper?"

"The what?"

"Hashtag Lake Dumper. It's all over social media. It was in the digital paper yesterday. It says he's tied to a major drug ring, that he disappears into thin air and that he is also a serial killer."

Nash shook his head. He hadn't had time to even think about the press, much less scroll through community posts about the case. "You know you can't believe everything on there, right?"

Maeve looked at him as if *he* was the teenager. "No, but where there's a hashtag, there's a story." Maeve wasn't yet sure what she wanted to do if she went into the navy, but he'd place his wager on Intelligence or JAG Corps. She was as stellar a writer as a negotiator.

"Keep it under your hat that I'm on it, okay?"

"Of course."

Aunt Clara walked into the room. "There's the puppy snatcher."

"Aunt Clara, thank you so much for helping me out here. I really appreciate it." He hugged and kissed her. "What the heck are you talking about, 'puppy snatcher'?"

"Noel Larson's mother was down at the café, spouting off about how her son's dogs were stolen. She doesn't know me from Adam, or rather Eve, but I paid attention in case it's something you could use. I know those Larson boys are up to no good. They've never had a good reputation. Neither did their grandfather."

"I appreciate you trying to help, but like I just told Maeve, you can't believe everything you hear." One thing about a small town was that word traveled fast, but it could often be misleading. "Where's Uncle Jim?"

"He went to check on our house and get us some more clothes. The nights have been cold and I wanted my flannel pj's."

"Is the woodstove working okay?" He walked over to the stove in the middle of the large living room.

"It's fine, but you know we don't like to leave it burning overnight. We've gotten used to our gas heat, let me tell you."

Gas heat was something Nash wanted to add to the house, but until the girls got situated with college and he knew how much it would be out-of-pocket for him, he was holding off. If Maeve's appointment to the Academy came through, he'd have more than enough for both boys' educations and to upgrade the house.

"There are down blankets in each of the bedroom closets." The last thing he wanted was for his relatives to be the least bit uncomfortable. They were sacrificing so much to help him out and always had. "I don't know what I'd do without you and Uncle Jim to help me. I wouldn't be able to keep my position as a K9 officer without you."

"We're family. It's what we do. Speaking of K9, where's Greta? You didn't leave her in the car, did you?"

"No, she's back at the clinic. Dr. Colton is keeping an eye on her. She got a minor injury this morning and needs a little TLC."

"Greta's okay, right?" Jon walked into the room,

grabbed an apple off the counter and bit into it, all while quizzing Nash. "I miss her the most. Not that we don't miss you."

"Gee, thanks, bud. Come over here and let me wrestle you."

Jon, thirteen, had started to eat like a horse and had grown four inches this past summer. He got close enough to Nash to lean in for a brief hug. Something in Nash's heart twinged with regret. As tough as the last five years had been, they had also passed in the blink of an eye. The kids were getting older and didn't need his constant care. Sure, the teenage years meant he had to stay present and vigilant, but it was nothing compared to the first crazy years of meal after meal, helping with homework, the chauffeuring. Paige had picked up a lot of the slack with the driving lately, and soon Maeve would be able to, too.

"I miss you guys."

"Miss you, too."

"But?"

"We love having Aunt Clara and Uncle Jim here. She made us cookies last night."

"That's what they really like about me." Aunt Clara laughed from the kitchen, where she was making herself a cup of tea. "Can I get you a coffee?"

"No, I have to get back."

"Are you staying at the station overnight?" Jon lifted the lid on the cookie jar and grabbed a handful of the cookies Aunt Clara had baked.

"Whoa on all those sweets—how about leaving some

for your brother and sisters? And no, I'm not staying at the station. I'm staying with Dr. Colton, actually."

"Patience?" Maeve's eyebrow rose in query.

"Yes." He waited for the firing squad.

"She's a fox!" Trey exclaimed, his face reddening.

"She's so nice. She let me help train the dogs the last family day." Maeve's thoughtful expression warmed his heart.

"Way to go, Nash." Jon held up his hand, waiting for his to fist-bump.

"Hold it right there. I'm staying with her as part of my job. There's a big case going on with the clinic, and besides adding some extra protection, I'm gathering evidence." A twist of the truth, but he had to keep his siblings off the trail they always focused on: finding him a girlfriend. Or, worse, a wife. He chalked it up to wanting a more permanent mother figure in their lives, but as Paige and Maeve matured, they seemed genuinely interested in his well-being. Sweet, but unwarranted. He was a bachelor.

After enjoying an early dinner with them and having a few words with Paige when she came home from swim practice, Nash headed out. He still had one more stop before the cabin.

Chapter 12

After a long day that included Nash's dive, Greta's injury and the Larson twins, Patience enjoyed the peaceful respite of the cabin. She'd paid heed to Nash's insistence that she take every precaution to make sure she wasn't followed. She hated the constant feeling of being watched that had plagued her since the night of the crime.

As she walked Greta around the clearing, she remained alert to every sound coming from the forest. The familiar birdsong as the sun began to set, the dropping leaves and pine needles, the chatter of squirrels that were still out and about, busily harvesting cones and acorns until the temperatures dropped low enough to signal winter's arrival. The thrum of an engine made

Greta alert, her posture frozen as she faced the source of the sound.

It had to be Nash. He'd texted he was on his way, but Patience's spine tingled and she struggled to draw a deep breath into her lungs. The tension of the last few days was getting to her.

When the familiar shape of his Jeep turned into the clearing, she let her shoulders relax. Greta's happy bark confirmed that her handler, Nash, was driving.

"Come on, girl. Let's go greet him."

Nash got out of the Jeep and Patience let herself enjoy the warmth that rolled over her, as easy as his long strides as he walked to her.

"Hey, Greta." He bent over and greeted his partner with unabashed affection. "How you feeling, girl?"

Greta wagged her tail, making her entire body wiggle.

"She's doing great. I think we'll get away without the cone of shame around her head. She hasn't made any attempt to paw at her wound."

"You're a smart girl, aren't you?" He straightened up and the light in his eyes had nothing to do with Greta's cut or how it was healing. The thrill that thrummed through Patience was undeniable. Nash was feeling the same attraction as she.

"I can't thank you enough for taking care of Greta today."

"I'm just glad you're both okay. That was a very scary situation you were in."

He nodded. "Yeah, it was. If the jerk had been any closer or stabbed Greta an inch or two deeper, it would have been a different outcome."

"That's not what I meant, Nash. You could have been killed."

"As you could have been, Patience, if I hadn't been there when the Larson twins stormed into the kennel, I'm not certain Noel wouldn't have assaulted you to take those dogs."

"Unlikely. I had the staff around, and he was on my turf."

"It's not about what either of us thinks, is it?" Nash stepped up next to her. "It's what we're feeling, why we're both worried about each other so much."

Was the great bachelor Nash Maddox going to admit he had feelings for her?

"It's only natural, I suppose." She didn't want to share her feelings, not completely, not yet. It was still early and hard to know if she was experiencing baby hormones, lust or early signs of something deeper and more lasting.

He smiled. "A baby changes everything, doesn't it? It's clear to me we're both worried whether or not the other is okay because we're so focused on the child's safety."

Tears sprang into Patience's eyes at the sting of his pronouncement. He'd been thinking about the pregnancy, and the baby's safety, which meant her safety, too. Not about her as an individual or possible partner. Before he could see the tears pooling she stepped away and headed back for the house.

"Patience, wait." He caught up to her on the porch. "What did I say?"

"Nothing, Nash. You said nothing. It's not important."

* * *

Nash couldn't ignore the tangle of emotions roiling in his gut. But even more, he couldn't brush off the obvious hurt and pain he saw his words had somehow caused Patience. He thought she wanted him to respect her need to be a single mom, and he'd just done that, hadn't he? Her eyes moved away, to his Jeep, and he followed her gaze.

"What's in the back of your car?"

"A few things I thought we'd need before long." Pride warred with trepidation as he tried to decipher her. "I'll bring them in later. We need to eat, and I'd like to make you one of my specialties."

"Oh?" Her eyes didn't look like she was about to break into sobs any longer, so that was a start.

"Pasta carbonara. The kids love it and it's quick. Plus it's really good with a bottle of cabernet. I know you can't have alcohol now, so I brought some sparkling grape juice."

"That's thoughtful of you."

"I've also got a few things to unload. Give me a bit of time and I'll get dinner going."

She didn't say anything, but retreated into the cabin and, he suspected, to her laptop, where he knew she spent dedicated time each evening entering her notes on patients and general clinic work. He hurried to the car and started to unload.

When he entered the cabin with the first of his goods, Patience was nowhere to be seen. Just as well, since he wanted to surprise her with everything. As he brought in the last of his purchases, she wandered back into the great room, her phone at her ear.

Her eyes widened at the pile of gifts he'd come bearing.

"I have to go, Layla. I'll call you back." She disconnected from her sister and turned her stunned eyes to him.

"What the hell is this supposed to be, Nash?"

Patience stared at the Christmas-size pile of baby products in front of the cabin's fireplace. She couldn't help herself from going to it, passing close enough to Nash to feel his body heat, but ignoring her instant physical reaction.

"You bought all of this on your own?"

"Yes."

Nash was raising his siblings, but they'd all been beyond baby and toddler stages when their parents had died. A high chair, baby swing, car seat. Diapers, baby wipes and a baby wipe warmer. A huge box with *Baby Spa* printed on it depicted a fancy tub complete with a shower faucet and jets. And there were other items she couldn't see, on the far side of the pile. She looked at him.

Nash stood behind the sofa, framed by the fading daylight that streamed in through the picture window. His face was partially in shadow, so it was hard to tell what he thought, or to see any hint of his motive for buying out the single Red Ridge baby supply store.

"Why, Nash? You know, the baby's not bigger than a peach right now."

He stepped into the light, his hazel eyes bright with intent, but she still wasn't sure. Why had Nash gone to this trouble?

"I'm a planner, Patience. It's part of why I like working with the K9 unit so much. It's about more than me or my skills. I have to train Greta every day and do the monthly training to keep us both at top form. I've kept my household running for the past five years, with all four siblings' schedules and my workload. The only way I've done it is by having a plan for everything. A baby is no different. It needs routine. The other thing I've learned is that the right tool for the job is essential." He paused to shake his head and chuckle. "When I was living on my own, before my parents' accident, I had a few plates, one pot, and I was the master of microwave cooking. But kids need three solid meals a day and frozen meals weren't going to cut it. I moved back into my parents' house and found that the kitchen was like driving a Cadillac after using a bicycle."

"But you don't have to do this. I already told you, I'm prepared to raise the baby myself."

"You haven't heard me, Patience. I get it—there's been a lot going on since the Lake Killer. We haven't had time to be together and talk about our circumstance."

"You're calling my pregnancy a *circumstance*?"

"No, I'm referring to how we're going to handle the baby. You know this. What are you afraid of?"

His words lanced her resistance to him. When he closed the distance between them, she willingly went into his arms. Tears pricked at her lids for the second time since he'd come home, and she let herself lean against him and he held her tight. "I'm all over the place. It's the baby hormones, it's knowing a killer wants me dead, it's being confronted by Noel Larson. It's seeing that poor woman dropped into the freezing lake. And yet the most important thing that's happened is that I'm going to have a baby."

"It scared the heck out of me when you were in the clinic and they were coming after you," Nash murmured in response. "And when Noel Larson tried to bully you, it was all I could do to keep my cool."

His palms moved in circles between her shoulder blades and she yielded to his touch, wrapping her arms around his waist and pressing her cheek against his chest. He was a full head taller than her and they fitted together perfectly. His breathing and heartbeat were steady, another reassurance.

"I never felt more frightened than when it came over the emergency response system that you'd suffered a diving casualty. If anything had happened to you, the baby would never know its father, Nash."

She lifted her head to look at him at the same time he moved his hand to cup her jaw. The comforting vibe between them turned to sizzling heat in the blink of her tear-filled eyes, and a zing of awareness hit deep in her belly, pooling between her legs.

Nash must have seen the want in her eyes as he lightly kissed her lips. "Are we giving this a go, Patience?" His deep baritone stoked her need to a white-hot flash point.

"Oh, yes." When his mouth covered hers she stopped

thinking, stopped worrying about how they'd take care of the baby. Stopped revisiting the sheer terror that gripped her at the thought of anything happening to Nash. She embraced the moment, the very sexy, delectable moment.

His tongue was hot and insistent as he probed the depths of her open, willing mouth. His hands, so very talented, stroked her from her shoulders to her ass, and when he moved one hand to cup her breast, she groaned. She let go of his shoulders and lifted her top over her head. Nash unhooked her bra and his hot mouth seared a path from her throat to her nipple, his tongue stroking it from hard to throbbing. She ground her hips against his erection and he pressed back, his need as demanding as hers.

"My bedroom, Nash. Please."

Nash had never felt the need to please a woman the way he did Patience. Their first time together had lasted all night and he'd made sure she'd been satisfied, as he always did with his partners. The best lovemaking was two-way pleasure. Their lovemaking in the cabin the other day had been a release they'd both needed, and reassurance that their one-night stand hadn't been a passionate fluke.

This was different, on a whole other plane. As if Patience's physical response to him meant more than the fact they shared a smoking-hot chemistry.

Her room was pure Patience—feminine pale yellow walls, contemporary clean lines, the aroma of fresh flowers present but not overpowering. He shrugged out of his shirt as he stood facing her at the foot of the bed and unbuckled his belt. Patience grinned.

"Let me help you with that." She slipped his belt out of its loops and unzipped his pants. As he shoved them down, she shimmied out of her scrubs, revealing a grape-colored thong with a lacy front panel that revealed dark curls with the same hint of red as the hair that framed her face. He got rid of his boxers, freeing his erection.

Her hands wrapped around him and he closed his eyes, tilted his head back. "Patience." At this rate he was going to come before he had a chance to join with her, and that would be a pity. He needed to be one with her again.

Her hands shifted to his chest and he moaned in disappointment, until her hot mouth took him. She made him want to do everything he could possibly imagine with her, for her, to her. After he cried out a second time, she stood and gently pushed him onto the bed.

He moved backward on his elbows until he was at the headboard, watching her the entire time. Her breasts, full and luscious, swung in rhythm to her steps as her long, lean legs covered the distance to her end table in only a few strides.

She climbed onto the bed and lay next to him. He ran his hands through her hair, kissed her deeply. Her taste and scent were heady, clearing his mind of anything but his unending need for her. He pressed her back into the mattress, covering her with his body.

"Nash." She tried to grasp his length, but he brushed

her off, working his mouth and tongue on her skin, from her lips, her throat, lingering at her breasts.

"Not yet, babe." He suckled at her nipples, smiling against her smooth skin each time she groaned or cried out in clear delight. Tortuous pleasure; he knew it well with Patience. She always made him need her so much it hurt in its intensity.

"Nash, I need you inside me."

"Patience, Patience."

He licked the valley around her navel, marveling at the soft curves where her belly had been washboard flat the first time they'd made love. It had been a detractor to him when women he dated, never seriously, alluded to having a family. He'd had no desire to be anything but a bachelor, and was holding out for all his siblings to be raised. Yet the physical evidence of Patience's pregnancy, with a baby they'd made together, took his desire for her to a level he'd never experience before. It was a hunger, this need for the beautiful woman in his arms.

He took in the very essence of her, and when he placed his mouth over her she writhed and gently moved her hips as he tasted her.

He'd never satisfy his hunger for Patience.

Patience thought that Nash's mouth on her nipples had been the single most sensual thing she'd ever known. Until he moved to the pulsing spot between her legs and devoured her with his hot, wet, eager mouth. There was no room for thoughts of anything but Nash, her need and the hope for mind-blowing fulfillment.

The orgasm came fast and hard as he licked her,

and she screamed her release even as she reached for him, wanting more. Nash didn't fight her this time but knelt between her legs, his arousal insistent against her quaking center.

"Nash, please." She arched her hips, unwilling to wait a second more.

"Babe." He thrust into her, stretching her wide and filling her depths with heat that reached to her soul. They moved in perfect unison, their bodies resuming the pace that was uniquely theirs.

Nash's skin became slick with sweat and she loved that she made him want to work so hard for her, loved that he fought to please her each and every time. With him she was able to let go of any inhibitions she'd ever had and just be herself, let her body do what it needed to do for completion.

Her release started in a low, forceful wave that rose to an untenable pitch until she shattered, shouting in pleasure with a breathless effort. Nash kept moving for a few more seconds, until he cried out, her name echoing about her room.

"We make a good team." Nash stroked her throat, ran his hand down her rib cage, over her hip as they lay face-to-face, coming down from their most recent sexcapade. He knew it was more, that this wasn't anything like the one-nighters he'd pulled with different women over the last five years.

His "sexual maintenance" dating had ended with that night with Patience. And now this.

She smiled in the dim light, two flickering battery candles making the room the perfect backdrop for such a sexy woman. "We are at that. When we're working together."

He shoved himself up into a seated position, his back against the headboard. Patience followed suit. "About that. I'm not asking you to commit to me, or anything like that. But I'm going to be an active father for the baby. It's not in my being to ignore a child I've fathered."

She looked at him, stroked his cheek. He needed to shave, but had loved rubbing his five o'clock shadow against the insides of her dewy thighs. "This is what's so attractive about you, Nash. You always want to do the right thing."

"But? I hear the 'but.'"

"But you need to be practical. You're a hard-core bachelor. You said so yourself the night we got together. In five, six years you'll be free of raising your siblings."

"A lot has changed since we met. Since that night."

"Well, yeah. I'm pregnant."

He shook his head. "It's more than that. You and I— we've gotten closer. Don't you feel it?"

She wouldn't meet his eyes and he held his breath. He'd pushed too far. And while it should concern him that he was actually trying to prove to Patience that he wanted anything but freedom from being a father, it didn't. It felt right.

"I don't know, Nash. What you said—about a lot having changed since we met. It's true. And I so appreciate that you're already preparing for the baby's arrival. But it's at least six months off, and then there'll be so much round-the-clock care that it's a tough time to try to figure out what either of us is going to do. I don't know how I'll be as a mother, but I do know I'm going to give it my best shot."

"That's all I'm asking you for, you know. I need you to give me and the idea of us co-parenting a decent shot."

She met his gaze and beyond her trepidation he saw a glimmer of hope. Maybe the seed of trust. "I'll try."

"That's all we can ever do."

A low growl sounded in the front of the cabin and they both sat up.

"Does she normally growl at deer or wildlife?" Patience's hopeful question was laced with trepidation.

"No." Nash's inner alarm screeched. Greta's abilities rarely failed him. There was an intruder on the property.

Chapter 13

Greta's sharp bark cracked through the air and Nash was up and dressed with his weapon in hand in under fifteen seconds. Patience's eyes widened, but she didn't show any signs of panic. She rolled toward the nightstand, where she'd put a gun safe, and punched in four numbers, unlocking it. When he saw the .45 in her hand, he motioned toward her clothes, strewed on the floor.

"Put those on and only come out after I tell you it's clear."

Greta's barks grew more insistent and he shoved his feet into his shoes, then put on his body armor. There was no telling who or what was on the other side of the cabin door.

"I'm going with you. Greta can guard the house. She can't go back out on patrol with her cut."

"You are not going anywhere. Do you have any body armor with you?"

She shook her head. "This weapon and the gun safe are all I took from my office."

"Then you do not leave this room. No matter what, Patience." He couldn't argue with her. There was an intruder and he had to take care of it.

Patience waited until she heard Nash shout and the front door open and close. Then she carefully crept into the short hallway and headed for the main room, her weapon in front of her as she cleared every nook and cranny in the cabin on her way forward. Just like her veterinary trauma training, the police training enabled her to perform as though she did this all the time.

Greta mostly maintained her alert stance at the front door, but once or twice paced to the picture window, which looked out onto total darkness.

Patience heard voices and Greta barked, two sharp, deliberate sounds. She jerked, unable to control her reaction. In the confines of the cabin, the big dog's vocalization sounded like a thunderclap.

She heard more voices as she waited, her weapon pointed at the door. With slow, deliberate steps she approached the kitchen sink and island counter and sank to her knees, using the granite surface for support. Anyone who walked into the cabin would have to get past her gunfire.

Three loud bangs sounded on the front door. Patience steadied her aim.

"Patience, it's Nash. I'm coming in."

Okay, so why didn't he just do so? She wouldn't shoot him.

The front door opened as Greta watched, and the dog didn't bark or whine. But Nash was behind a man Patience knew too well. She stood and lowered her pistol.

"Daddy."

Fenwick Colton's face was partially obscured by the custom cowboy hat he wore, always a part of his wardrobe no matter if he was in sweatpants or a tuxedo. Tonight he was in his usual business suit with a lariat. The sterling silver hawk bolo tie at the base of his collar was his signature symbol. The raptor suited him, as she'd never known her daddy to be anything but focused and predatory.

"Hey, short stuff. Since when do you have your own personal guard?" He shoved a thumb over his shoulder, indicating Nash.

"What are you doing here, Daddy? You could have been killed by either one of us." Typical of Fenwick, he hadn't called first. If he wanted to see her, he just showed up on his own timetable. Although he usually asked her to come to the office or stop by his estate. And almost always passed the message through Layla.

Concern ratcheted Patience's tension tenfold. "Oh, no, is it Layla? Is she okay?"

"What? Of course she's okay. At least she was when I left the office almost an hour ago. Right before I came here. I forgot how crazy the turns are. Next time I'll drive my four-wheel drive."

"How did you know I was here?" Layla must have told him, but Patience wanted to hear it from him.

Fenwick loved nothing more than playing "I've got a secret," being a disciple of the "knowledge is power" school since forever. If he'd found out she or her siblings were in trouble, or more likely planned to get themselves in trouble, when they were teens, he'd lord the information over them for the remainder of the time they lived at home.

"Layla mentioned it. She said you needed some space, so I didn't expect this young man to be here. You okay, fella?" Fenwick looked at Nash with genuine concern.

Nash remained silent, but Patience was pretty certain she sensed the heat of his frustration and anger, for his eyes sparked and his mouth was pressed in a frown.

"You should have called first, Daddy. We've been over this." And they had. She'd told him not to visit her at her small townhome unless he called and they had standing plans. Same for the cabin. Fenwick thought the world revolved around him and paid little heed to his children's, or their guests', concerns. Not that she'd had a lover over lately, but Patience valued her personal space.

"Do you have any bourbon?" Her father walked into the cabin. "And why the heck are you flashing a gun at me, Patience?"

She sighed and put the weapon on the counter. She opened the cabinet over the refrigerator. "I think I still have the bottle you brought with you the last time you were here." And the only time. Fenwick had checked out the cabin when she'd built it, but that was it. She found the bottle of his favorite drink and poured him two fingers.

"Here you go, Daddy." She placed it on the island and saw that Nash had quietly come in and closed the door. Greta lay against it, back to her preferred location.

"Aren't you going to join me?" Fenwick looked at her, and she saw how little he'd aged over the years since she'd left home. No wonder he never had a problem finding a date or his next wife.

"No, but I'll have a ginger ale." She caught Nash's glance and saw the surprise. Had he thought she'd told her family? Only Layla knew about the baby.

"How about you—what did you say your name was?"

"Nash. Nash Maddox. And I'm afraid I have to pass, too, as I'm on an active case. I'm with the RRPD."

"Haven't we met? I have a few relatives on the force." Fenwick's attention went to Greta. "She's beautiful."

"And a K9, too." Nash looked like he'd rather converse with a billy goat.

"Thank you for the work you do. Red Ridge is lucky to have such a fine police department, and we have the best K9 facility in South Dakota." Fenwick's skinny chest puffed at his boast. He'd funded most of the recent upgrades at the training center and clinic. And now Colton Energy faced bankruptcy.

"The training center is vital to the county's security, Daddy." Patience couldn't help the verbal prod. He threatened to cut off funding whenever Colton Energy hit a rough patch, which she found stressful and unnecessary.

"Of course it is, but you know that if I don't keep my

company going, I won't have anything to give. No worries, though. Your sister Layla is a true Colton." He held up his drink to Patience, then nodded to Nash. "Cheers."

"Cheers." She and Nash toasted with their sodas, but all she wanted to do was throw her drink in her father's face. It wasn't like she wasn't used to his self-centered ways, but his high-handed manner was over-the-top, even for him. For him to throw Layla's willingness to marry the creepy Hamlin around like a badge of honor made Patience sick.

After he took a healthy swallow, Fenwick looked around the kitchen and living room. "I forgot how excellent a job you did on the renovation. This is a very nice getaway for you."

"Why are you really here, Daddy?" She knew how to pin him down after years of practice. Fenwick didn't even bother to feign ignorance, or pretend he'd come on a friendly visit.

"You know about your cousin Demi, right? The trouble she's in?"

"Of course I do. But which part are you talking about?" Demi Colton had been branded by the town as the most likely candidate to be the Groom Killer. The first victim, Bo Gage, had been her fiancé until he'd left her for Hayley Patton. The breakup gave Demi motive, along with some circumstantial evidence. Her name had been written in the first victim's blood by his body, and a piece of her jewelry had been found near the crime scene. Plus, more than one witness put her at a few of the murder sites. But Patience liked Demi, and if her gut was correct, Demi was innocent. A couple months before she'd fled, Demi had brought in an injured animal for Patience to care for, and her demeanor bespoke her compassion and integrity. Not the characteristics of a serial killer.

"You know very well I'm talking about the Groom Killer herself. Demi Colton." Fenwick took another hefty swig before pointing his finger and glass at Nash. "Your colleagues need to get their crap together and arrest her. What the hell is taking you all so long? Now we have a second murderer on our hands."

Before Nash could respond, Fenwick turned back to Patience. "Finn filled me in." No apology, no expression of concern for her well-being. *Typical Daddy.*

She saw Nash's spine stiffen and for a second Patience thought he might answer Fenwick with some hard words of his own.

"You're right, Mr. Colton. It's a team effort, and the RRPD is working around the clock on this case. We'll catch the murderer, sooner than later."

"'Sooner' is not soon enough. How many more innocent victims will it take? Demi's clearly the one you want. What's keeping you from bringing her in for questioning? She's been spotted enough in town that no matter where she's hiding out, it can't be too far away. Do I have to remind you that you're speaking to the mayor of Red Ridge?"

"No, sir. But obviously you need reminding that as mayor, you need to discuss this with the chief of police." A muscle strained in Nash's jaw. Her father needed to leave.

"Daddy, did you come all this way because you knew

Nash was here with me? This is a crappy way to throw your weight around." Nash might not want to dress her father down, but nothing kept her from doing it.

She was glad she'd kept Demi's K9 clinic visit to herself. It wasn't relevant to the case in any way except to challenge the stance that Demi was a rough-around-the-edges hothead. Demi's brothers on the RRPD were in her corner, at least.

Patience only hoped Demi and her baby were okay—she'd been pregnant when she'd fled town and had had the baby on the run. That couldn't have been easy. Just last month Demi had been spotted in town, in disguise, with her baby in a carrier. Patience hoped the real killer would be caught soon so that Demi and her infant could come out of the shadows.

"I heard you were living up here for the time being, yes." He glared at Nash. "And I was told she had the finest K9 team with her. Now I'm not so sure."

Nash didn't reply with words. His own glare said it all. Patience almost laughed at how her father actually balked. Fenwick Colton wasn't used to being shut down by someone he considered a subordinate. Even though no RRPD officer worked directly for him, he acted as if they did and didn't have a problem putting pressure on Finn to keep or fire officers on a whim. As mayor, it was in Fenwick's purview to do so. Fortunately, Finn was a man of integrity and usually able to keep Fenwick mollified, while not letting the mayor's opinions negatively affect the RRPD.

"Daddy, it's going to take you the better part of an hour to get home. I know you've had a long day. Why don't you have a bite to eat, then head out?" Fenwick was an early bird and she hoped he'd take the hint. She didn't want him driving right after downing the scotch, though, so she brought out some cheese and crackers.

"I wanted to know you were safe, daughter. Don't believe me, but it's true. At least you're in a secure location, save for the woods. Though a man would have to be crazy to try to scale the mountain to get here on foot." He munched on the snack.

"You know I've got cameras all over the place." She mentally kicked herself for not checking the security system's monitor before Nash ran out to find her father. They wouldn't have been so worked up and would have seen it was him.

"The murderer you saw on the lake followed you to your town house, I heard. So you two decided to hole up here?" Daddy was a dog with a bone. He thrived on details.

"Not exactly." As she replied, Fenwick got up from the island stool and walked around, looking at the place. He wasn't one to sit still for long.

Still energetic and wire thin, he never had a shortage of women who wanted to be with him. She and Layla had compared notes and agreed their father wasn't going to have a fourth wife. He saw potential mates as future divorce adversaries—money grabbers. And Patience would like to think he was afraid of another broken heart, though he never displayed anything that indicated it.

"Nice touch with the gas insert." Fenwick stalled, and for the first time Patience wondered if he wasn't a little lonely. Unless he had a date on his arm, he went home alone to the expansive mansion she'd grown up in.

He stood in front of the fireplace, then turned to look out the picture window, where the porch lights illuminated the Appalachian chairs and rocker. "And the porch looks like a nice place to start the day."

"It is…" She almost choked on her words as she saw the huge pile of baby supplies beneath the window. She'd forgotten about Nash's shopping spree.

Her father's hawkish gaze missed nothing. When he turned to face her, he assessed her, pausing when he got to her belly. Incredulity and comprehension played across his features.

"What's with the kid stuff, Patience?"

Patience swallowed as she faced down the first adversary she'd ever known.

Chapter 14

Nash wished Fenwick Colton would magically disappear. Why couldn't the man see his daughter as the beautiful woman she was? Instead, he treated her like she was his possession. *Enough.*

"I brought the supplies here. They're mine." Nash spoke up, seeing the consternation on Patience's face. Her cheeks were flushed and she bit her lower lip so deeply he expected to see blood. The least he could do was buy her time. If she didn't want to tell her powerful father that she was pregnant, he'd lie.

"Can I ask why?" Fenwick looked from Patience to Nash, then back to his daughter. She waited for Nash to meet her gaze, and when he did she nodded. She raised her chin and squarely faced her father.

"Daddy, you're going to be a grandfather."

Silence fell in tense shards, and Nash fought to think of something he could say or do to ease the stress he knew this caused Patience. She'd turned to him that first night they were together because she'd had a blowup with Fenwick and Layla. Something to do with Fenwick's business floundering and Layla agreeing to marry Hamlin Harrington, two things Patience believed were related. She blamed her father for pushing her sister to marry the much older businessman. Nash didn't want to get in the middle of family stuff; he had enough of his own. But the baby in Patience's belly was his.

Fenwick Colton and he were family by default. Holy hell, he'd never taken the time to think about that. His thoughts, his heart hadn't gone past Patience. And the baby.

"Well, I'll be damned. Congratulations!" Fenwick rounded the breakfast bar and took his daughter in what Nash thought was a genuine hug. Patience looked a little stiff, but she did hug him back. It was a start. When Fenwick released her, he looked at Nash. "I take it you're responsible?"

"We're both responsible for the baby, Daddy. I don't have to tell you how it works." Patience blushed and Nash bit back a laugh.

"No. No, you don't." Fenwick eyed Nash. "What are you going to do about it? As far as raising the child? My grandchild." Of course, Fenwick immediately claimed the unborn babe, another possession.

"Patience and I are working out the details." He walked over to her so that they'd face Fenwick together.

But her dad wasn't accusatory. He seemed bemused.

"Is that why you're here together? Besides keeping safe from the Lake Killer. You're figuring things out?"

"We're assigned to the same case, Daddy. I work with the RRPD on any K9 operation, technically, but this one is requiring extra time."

Fenwick gave his daughter a look that Nash knew probably melted his opponents in the boardroom. Patience stood her ground, and Fenwick turned to Nash.

"You're responsible for her now."

Nash saw red. Patience wasn't a commodity to be traded for a dowry. He refused to raise the tension in the room, though. And truth be told, he did feel responsible for Patience and the baby's safety.

"I'm responsible for me, Daddy." Patience certainly had the dog-with-a-bone DNA in her, too.

Fenwick waved his hand at both of them. "I would have preferred you did this the old-fashioned way, getting married first. But I also wanted you to join the family business instead of going to vet school." In what Nash suspected was a rare admission, the elder Colton's face fell as he contemplated his daughter. "And look at me. Two divorces, the awful, tragic loss of your mother, five kids, and I've not done well by you or your brothers and sisters. Who am I to say what's best?"

"Daddy, you did the best you knew how to do at the time. And we've all turned out okay, haven't we?"

Fenwick nodded. "That you have. Congratulations, my dear." He kissed Patience on the forehead, and Nash saw that she seemed reserved after such an emotional display by her father. This wasn't a family used to outward expressions of affection.

"Nash." Fenwick stretched his hand out and Nash shook it. "All I ask is that you do right by my daughter and grandchild."

"Yes, sir."

"Keep yourselves safe from the Lake Killer. And I mean business about the Groom Killer, Nash. The RRPD needs to get Demi behind bars. Red Ridge needs its sense of security back. We need people to feel safe to get married again."

"Is your father always such a prick?" Nash sat on the sofa next to her. Patience had distracted herself from her father's surprise visit by opening the pile of baby supplies after he departed.

"This is like Christmas, Nash. How did you know which swing to buy? I was at a friend's baby shower a while ago and she received four different swings, each supposedly the best." Patience hadn't paid attention to the discussion of timers and wireless controls. She'd dismissed it as useless information. "You know you've purchased the top-of-the-line swing, right? This has not only a timer but also a Wi-Fi speaker so that you can customize the baby's music. And it says here that the speakers will not exceed safe decibel levels." She pored over the service manual.

Nash's strong hands covered the text. "Answer my question, Patience. Do you think how your father behaved was appropriate?"

"Which part? How he arrogantly assumed we'd both do his bidding and work to get Demi arrested? Or how he threw his usual barb at me for being a 'mere' veterinarian and not working for the high-and-mighty Colton legacy?"

Nash looked at her with compassion sprinkled with a little bit of surprise.

"You're an amazing woman, you know that? I don't mean to put down your family, but it's fair to say that your father is a known entity in Red Ridge. You don't fit in his world, Patience. Money isn't your be-all and end-all. I get it. I have degrees in finance and computer science. I could have used my siblings as an excuse to follow through with my postcollege plans and gone to San Francisco or Chicago to get a moneymaking job. Bring in the bucks for my siblings, focus on their financial future. My aunt and uncle would have taken them in."

"So why didn't you?"

"Because I'm made of the same stuff you are. I knew the kids needed their closest family member, their half brother, more than they needed trust funds and college accounts."

"What made you pick law enforcement?"

"I was interested in white-collar crime and was beefing up my résumé with security jobs for high-end corporations. But it was too sterile for me. I wanted, needed, to work with real people every day. And I've always loved dogs, so K9 was a natural fit. I had just graduated the police academy when my folks were killed."

"Talk about divine timing."

"Yeah, it was, in an awful way. I had a regular paycheck from the get-go. And in total disclosure, the kids aren't without college funds. There was a life insurance policy that provided enough for each of them to attend a state school. Paige and Maeve are on the scholarship track, though, so the sky's the limit for where the boys will go to university."

His pride in his siblings touched her. "You're a wonderful father, Nash."

"Big brother, you mean. Yeah, I'm their parent, four times over. But I've had help. Besides my aunt and uncle, there are so many other family members and friends of my parents who've stepped up. My folks each had two siblings—that's a lot of babysitting power right there." He grinned, making what he did seem easy.

"I don't know how you've done it. Watch hours, duty assignments... They aren't all family-friendly."

"I haven't done anything anyone else wouldn't have." Nash's modesty made him all the more attractive.

"Give me a break. You've gone above and beyond and you know it."

"Which begs the question, Patience. Are you going to let me participate fully as the baby's father?" His question jarred her out of the bubble she wanted to stay in. Where she didn't have to make a big decision, where her heart wasn't at stake. Where a mad killer hadn't drawn a bright bloodred target on her back.

"Is this really the time to talk about it? There's a serial killer out there, another killer after me and the Larson twins after both of us. Why don't we get through the next few weeks and to the point where, hopefully, the Groom Killer is stopped and whoever I saw on the lake is apprehended? The Larson twins aren't stupid enough to come after us directly, but they might send their own thugs. To figure out how we'll manage the parenting—it's just a lot to take in."

"Come here." Nash opened his arms and Patience sidled up to him on the sofa, loving the unwavering strength he so freely gave her. Once her head was nestled on his shoulder, he spoke as he stroked her hair.

"Neither of us planned this, Patience. After these last days together, I'd say we have an attraction that doesn't come along every day. You don't want to settle down— I understand completely understand that, neither of us wanted to. It's okay to enjoy one another, draw fortitude from our bond, though, isn't it? And the baby will do better if his or her parents get along."

"I can't argue with that, but it's not that simple, Nash." She ignored the disappointment when he admitted he didn't want to settle down, either. And she wasn't ready to correct his assumption that she hadn't changed her mind about it, either. All she could think of was the fight she had in front of her to balance her career and impending mommydom. She'd fought long and hard to achieve independence from her father and the darker side of the Colton legacy, only to find out the K9 clinic in her mother's name was under threat of closure. "We have to catch the Lake Killer and the Groom Killer." As she said the words, she still couldn't get her head wrapped around the fact that two murderers were on the loose in Red Ridge.

"Speaking of that, I have some updates from Finn. I didn't want to say anything in front of your father. We believe the Lake Killer is an operative for a North American heroin and fentanyl distribution ring. He's an expert at disguises and disappearing as needed. We're getting closer to him, Patience."

She shivered. "I hate being so close to such evil, Nash."

"I know. Let me do the heavy lifting, worrywise, for you. The only thing you have to concern yourself with is staying safe and healthy. Trust me as your friend to take care of the rest for you."

"You can't charm your way out of this one, Officer Maddox." She playfully punched his jaw. His stubbled, sexy jaw.

He caught her fingers in his teeth and his tongue circled the tips, shooting mind-numbing awareness to the spot between her legs.

"Who said anything about charm?" He tugged on the tendril of hair he'd been playing with until their lips met. Patience had no argument. The next days and weeks would be scary until they caught both killers. She'd take comfort in the security of Nash's arms while she could.

The next week Patience drove to her prenatal checkup with a combination of nervousness and hope in her belly. She laughed as she realized something else existed inside her—the baby. Was it a boy or girl? She and Nash were minutes from finding out.

As much as she tried to convince herself she could do all of this on her own, she was excited to know Nash would be here, would see the baby for the first time with her.

It was hard to imagine life before, without Nash, and

now it was impossible to conceive that he wouldn't always be at her side, as their child was born and then grew over the years.

Her heartbeat sped up and it wasn't from distress. Maybe it would have a year, six months ago. Before she'd been with Nash. She was a different woman, with a fresh perspective on life and the importance of appreciating those who meant the most.

Nash was definitely in that category.

She spotted Nash's car in the ob-gyn's parking lot and pulled up next to it. Nash rose to his feet when she entered the reception area, a copy of *Your Baby* in his hands. The sight of such a big strong man holding a magazine about babies made her smile. And then tears formed in her eyes.

"Patience. What?" Nash stood in front of her, clutching the periodical.

She shook her head, wiped her eyes. "Nothing. Hormones. I'll get checked in—give me a minute."

As soon as she'd given her insurance information she sat beside Nash, clipboard in hand.

"You have to fill that whole page out?" Nash eyed the questionnaire.

She fanned the multipage document. "More like three pages. The doctor needs to know my entire history, plus how I'm feeling."

"And how are you feeling?" His concern touched her and she fought tears again.

"I'm good." Grateful. Hopeful. But hopeful for what? That the baby enjoyed perfect health? Or that

Nash might actually be a permanent part of her, and the baby's, life?

"Patience?" He refused to allow her off the hook that easily.

"It's just the hormones. And let's face it, we've had a lot going on." She looked around the room at the other waiting mothers, in various stages of pregnancy. She kept thinking she looked the same as usual, but in fact, anyone could see she was pregnant. Her belly was fuller and starting to protrude like a basketball.

"We have." His tone matched hers—low and measured. But still, there were plenty of ears to catch their conversation and this wasn't the place for police talk.

Her hand paused over the question about family history. "Nash, do you know if anyone in your family had any birth defects, or congenital disease?"

His brow furrowed. "Not that I know of. All of my half siblings are healthy as horses, as you've seen. Since I don't have a biological full sibling, I don't know about anyone but me, and from what my dad told me, my mother had no problems with my birth. She died when I was a teen, long after their divorce. I'd lived with both of them on an alternating schedule up until her death. My dad remarried a year later, and he and my stepmom had all four kids pretty quickly."

"I'm sorry, Nash." Patience had never thought to ask him about his parents and why his dad had remarried. And now all three parental figures in his life had passed. "The baby must mean that much more to you."

"You understand that better than me." His gaze left

hers and he looked around the waiting room. "We'll talk about it later."

"Yes." She finished filling out the form and realized she'd underestimated how much could go wrong with a pregnancy. As a medical professional herself, working with animals, she understood the basics. But she hadn't taken the time to apply it to her situation, to her baby.

"Ms. Colton?"

"That's Dr. Colton." Nash spoke up and Patience blushed. The nurse looked at her file.

"I'm sorry, Dr. Colton. Follow me."

Patience stood, and with Nash at her side walked into the examination room, where they'd find out how their baby fared.

Nash hoped like heck that Patience didn't see how freaking nervous he felt. Thankfully, she couldn't see his sweating palms, or feel how tight the muscles in his chest clamped down on his rib cage. He'd watched countless canines whelp pups, and he dealt with kids on a daily basis. But his siblings weren't babies and puppies were…pups. Not a human baby with an entire life in front of it. His father and stepmother had made it look so easy when the kids were young, when the house was a complete cacophony of toddlers and babies. He'd come in later, when they were old enough to dress themselves and eat from a plate.

"Do I need to put on a robe?" Patience appeared fine, her usual confident self, except for the way she kept biting her lower lip. At this rate she'd gnaw it off before they got to the ultrasound part.

"No, that isn't necessary. You'll pull your waistband down so that the doctor can measure you, and then he'll put some gel on it for the ultrasound. That's it. Are you interested in knowing the sex of the baby?"

Patience's gaze flew to Nash's. "What do you think?"

He gulped. "I don't know. I guess it's a good idea, to be prepared."

"But the surprise of finding out at birth might make it more fun, more to look forward to."

The nurse cleared her throat. "I'll let you two talk about it while you're waiting for the doctor. He had a late delivery last night—early this morning, actually—so we're running about fifteen minutes behind. We'll be back shortly." She left the room.

After Patience scooted up onto the exam table, Nash sank into the chair. His knees never wobbled, never behaved like jelly. Did all new fathers-to-be go through this?

"Nash, are you okay?" Patience's concern pierced his nerves.

"Yeah, I'm good. I'm not the one carrying our kid in my belly. You're the one we need to focus on."

"It's not just about me, Nash. Yes, the baby and I are in this together. But you're the dad. It's okay if you're feeling shaky about it."

"It's not because I already am raising four kids, Patience. I'm not disappearing on you. I'm in this for the long haul." Annoyance made his temples pound. He hated it when she fell back upon her belief that he wanted nothing to do with more kids after he finished raising his siblings. Sure, he hadn't planned the pregnancy any more than she had, but it was what it was.

"I know you are. It's not a part-time dad who does all the research you've been doing, or who is so determined to equip the baby with the supplies you've purchased." She smiled from the exam table, her hand on her belly in a classically maternal pose. Her beauty made his heart hurt.

"The baby is going to be beautiful, Patience. Like you."

"Healthy is all that matters. And yes, the baby is already beautiful. We're going to see it today."

"I read that the first appointment is usually just a fetal heartbeat check—it can be too early to see a whole lot."

"Yes, if we'd planned this and were here for the first time when I'd just missed my period. But this is two missed periods out, so I'm at least fourteen weeks along, maybe even sixteen. My periods have never been regular, so we'll have to see what the doc says."

"Do you want to know the sex, Patience?" It was her decision. Nash would love to know, but he wasn't the one who had labor and delivery to get through. Maybe she needed the surprise to wait.

She worried her lower lip again. "My instinct is yes, of course. I'm a K9 vet and it's my job to know what our bitches are having, their health, all we can find out before the pups are born. The baby isn't a puppy, though, is it?" She looked at him and he got up and went to her.

"Come here." He wrapped his arms around her and she leaned into him, her head on his chest.

"Thank you for coming today, Nash. It's so much to…"

"To absorb." He rubbed his lips on her hair, breathed in her ginger-spice scent.

"Yes. I keep telling myself I'm a professional and this is nothing unknown to me, except for the fact that I'm having the baby. But it's all uncharted territory. All those books with the pictures of the pregnant woman sitting in deep contemplation of her baby, they're stressing me out. I haven't had time to do anything but survive these last weeks."

"We're working on it, babe." He resolved to put the Groom Killer and Lake Killer in their rearview mirrors as soon as he humanly could. His work colleague, the mother of his child, deserved at least that much.

Wait—was Patience his partner only in work and making the baby, or more?

He shoved the questions down. Today was about their baby and figuring out what they needed to do next.

Three quick raps sounded before the door opened and Dr. Girard entered. "Dr. Colton and…"

"Nash. Nash Maddox." He shook the doctor's hand, and then Patience did.

"Dr. Girard."

"Well, congratulations to you both. Your urine test was positive, but you already knew that, I assume. I see you've missed two periods."

"Yes. There wasn't an open appointment before today, and the receptionist told me I could do a same-day walk-in sooner, but I've been involved in a case at work."

"You're the vet at the RRPD K9 facility, right?" He reached for his stethoscope. "There's been a lot of excitement in Red Ridge lately, according to the news. Breathe in." He continued the exam as he peppered her with questions. Nash's impatience grew, but then he figured out that the doctor was developing a rapport with Patience. He recognized it because it's what he did with citizens during his police work. Put them at ease, let them know they could trust you.

"That's me. And yes, we've been busy." Patience lay flat at the doctor's invitation and pushed her waistband down low. Dr. Girard pulled out a tape measure and ran it from her pubic bone to the top of the baby bump. "What am I measuring?" she asked.

The doctor smiled. "You're more than four months, from this, but let's see what the ultrasound says. This will be cold." Without further comment, he squirted clear gel onto her belly and fired up the ultrasound machine.

"Have you two decided if you want to know the sex?" He moved the paddle up and down Patience's belly, and Nash was torn between watching her expression and the image that began to take shape on the screen.

"Yes. Yes, we do," Patience answered, and Nash's stomach flipped. It was the same kind of anticipation he had while watching one of the kids participate in an athletic or academic event. Excitement for how it could turn out, joy at watching their achievement.

"Well, folks, here's the deal. You're measuring larger than a typical four-month fetus."

"It's not older than that—before this baby was conceived I hadn't had sex in at least a year." Patience's declaration brooked no reaction from the doctor, but Nash's insides tightened, then erupted in what he could only describe as a glow. She'd picked him to ease her loneliness with, as he had picked her.

"It's clear to me that you conceived when you think you did. The fact is, there's more than one baby here."

Patience almost sat up and grabbed the paddle from Dr. Girard.

"What? How many?"

"Two. You're having twins. And you're ready for the sex?" He narrowed in on one baby, and she stared at the screen. "Here's a boy."

Tears slid past her lids, and she blinked so that she wouldn't miss one bit of seeing her babies. *Her babies.* Nash's babies. She looked at him. His gaze was transfixed on the screen, and in the dim light she couldn't tell if he was especially pale or just reflecting the monitor.

"And here's a girl. So, fraternal twins, a boy and a girl. Both are measuring right where we want them to be."

"How have I been pregnant with twins and not realized it sooner?" She blurted out her thoughts before she had a chance to process.

"Good genes is my bet. And you're very healthy, active. It's easy to mistake a pregnancy for stomach upset, the flu or none of the above. The bottom line is that you're doing great and so are your babies." He wiped the gel from her belly and helped her to sit up.

"Will I be able to work until term?"

"We'll take it a week at a time, but my guess is no. With twins it can get tricky toward the last trimester, if not sooner. We want to keep your babies inside until we know their lungs are fully developed. Patience, you're doing great. Hopefully you'll be the mother who goes full-term without a hitch, besides getting uncomfortable the last few weeks. But we have to monitor you, the babies. If anything comes up that necessitates bed rest, then that's what we'll do. For now, enjoy it and be glad you're out of the woods for morning sickness. These next several weeks can be very exciting and a great time to get ready for the babies."

Patience listened with half a mind as the doctor reassured her. She couldn't stop looking at Nash, seeking the warmth of reassurance in his glance. But her search was in vain. He looked like a man with shell shock. More like twin shock.

Adding one child to the four he was raising was a tall order. Might twins be too much for even Nash's indomitable strength?

They walked out of the ob-gyn clinic together and Nash stood with her near the beat-up sedan. "We'll get through this, Patience." Sure, he was thrown off balance. Twins. Yet nothing, not one thing, was more important to him than her well-being. He had to make her see she wasn't alone in this.

Her teary eyes made his heart hurt. "Twins, Nash.

Two babies. There's no way you're going to be able to handle two in addition to your four siblings."

"Hey." He cupped her face. "That's my decision, not yours. All that matters is that you're healthy, the babies are healthy. That's it. We'll get the killers in no time, trust me. These past weeks will seem a blur, but they'll be over. And then we can live life the way we want to." He kissed her gently, not caring who saw.

As he drove away, he wondered if they'd agree to what kind of life they wanted for the babies. First, Red Ridge had to be safe from two murderers.

Chapter 15

Patience was used to coming in on weekends, as she did most days all year round since she'd started working at the clinic. But she had to admit that she'd gotten used to the life she and Nash had carved out in the cabin over the past weeks. Leaving the warmth of Nash's arms this morning had been difficult. He'd let her go alone because she was heading straight to the clinic, to a safe place. Fortifications around the fences and gates, as well as the entranceways, made it much more difficult for the Lake Killer, or any intruder, to get past.

She and Nash had fallen into a comfortable routine over the last few weeks since the ob-gyn appointment, with no further threats from the Lake Killer or the Larson twins. The ongoing threat never left her awareness, though.

As much as being with Nash each day and each sexy night made her want to believe it'd always be like this, Patience couldn't allow herself to grow complacent. She did let herself enjoy her work, though. Wearing extra roomy scrubs she'd purchased meant that, so far at least, no one had asked her if she was pregnant. If they did, would she tell them there were two? How could she not?

She'd had to move the monthly community-wide K9 training day to a Saturday. Red Ridge citizens signed up months in advance to learn from the K9 experts. But since Patience had spotted the Lake Killer, the workload and security requirements made training with civilians during the week nearly impossible. The RRPD was stretched thinner than ever.

She made the drive from the cabin in just under fifty minutes, thanks to the clear roads and lack of precipitation. She headed for the postoperative board to see which patients were still in-house, and then over to the kennels.

"*Good* morning!" Gabby, the parrot, stretched her red wings for Patience, begging for an affectionate beak rub from her. Patience complied, stroking the smooth surface, careful to keep her fingers clear of the edges of Gabby's marbled gray-and-white beak.

"Morning, Gabby. I've missed you, too."

The macaw made kissing noises, like two lips smacking together, and Patience laughed. "I'm not that stupid. You nicked me the last time you asked for a kiss, remember?"

"Hey, sister." Blake, her younger brother by two years, stood in the entrance.

"Hi, Blake. How are you doing? And where's Juliette?" Juliette's K9 partner, Sasha, had recently injured her paw, so the beagle was doing some light training with Patience before being cleared for regular sessions at the training center.

"They stopped just outside to say hi to someone, so I thought I'd come see you privately for a minute. Because the real question is, how are *you* doing?"

Patience straightened. Her brother's eyes and fair coloring matched their father's. He resembled Fenwick more than she did, but despite being wealthy in his own right, Blake couldn't be less like the selfish, money-seeking businessman.

"I'm fine. Let me guess. Dad's been bugging you?"

"No, but he did call me." She watched her brother's gaze fall to her belly. Her much-extended belly. She realized her baggy scrubs weren't cutting it. By her count she was almost eighteen weeks pregnant, and none of her jeans or fitted pants were able to be zipped up any longer. She'd have to make a general announcement soon.

"Yes, I'm pregnant. It's true. But what Daddy doesn't know yet, what I didn't know when I saw him, is that I'm having twins. What else did he tell you?"

Blake shook his head, a wide grin splitting his face. He enveloped her in a big bear hug. "Twins? That's great, Patience. Congratulations." When he let her go, he looked at her and she saw that he was sincere. No judgment or recrimination. Just joy.

"Thanks. I have to admit it's come as a surprise, but I'm getting more excited about it." She braved putting a palm on her belly. "And I guess I can't really hide it too much longer."

"No need to hide it. It's your life." Blake paused, his own hand on the door of an empty kennel. "It's none of my business, sis, but are you and the father, uh, an item?"

"Daddy didn't tell you who the father is?"

"He may have mentioned a certain K9 officer's name in between a string of cursing, yes."

They both laughed. Patience nodded. "Yes, Nash is my baby daddy. *Babies'* daddy. It's a boy and a girl. But don't get the wrong idea about Nash and me. He's insisting on being involved with the babies, but he's got four kids of his own to raise."

"I don't know Nash Maddox well, but I've met him a few times and he doesn't strike me as the type to blow smoke, Patience. He'll be there for you. Why wouldn't he?"

Because she wouldn't let him. Because she wanted to keep her independence. Because she needed her autonomy in all areas of her life. "You know I have a tough time with men, Blake."

"Aw, sis. Nash isn't our daddy. It's hard for us to see that there are men who really give a fig about their kids and are devoted to their wives. We didn't have that example. But there are good guys. Nash is one of them."

"How about you, Blake?"

His glance slid away. "I'm doing my best to be a good partner and father. Finally." He'd recently fallen for K9 officer Juliette Walsh, who'd had his child three years earlier. But Blake hadn't known about his kid until he and Juliette connected again. Patience knew it had been hard on all involved.

"You got your happy ending, Blake. I'm happy for you."

He nodded. "And you can have yours, too, sis."

Nash let the boys out of the Jeep and looked around the clinic's training yard. Patience stood with two other trainers, their attention on a pair of young pups that were joining the RRPD K9 team.

"Can Greta run with us?" Troy looked at Nash.

"No, but you can walk her over there on her leash." He let Greta out of the back and handed the lead to Troy. "Remember, she's your responsibility until you get her to Dr. Colton."

"Doc Patience lets us play with all the dogs."

"That's when you're here for a family day, or to help with the other clinic patients. This is an official K9 training session for dogs who've been under veterinary care. It's a privilege to be here."

"We heard you before." Jon was being a snarky teenager, which Nash could usually brush off. But today it annoyed him.

"Watch your tone, Jon."

"Sorry." The teen's mumble felt like a victory. Nash had been through such emotional upheaval with Paige and Maeve when they were that age. So far the boys seemed so much easier to handle. but he knew that one wrong, impulsive decision on their part could change the whole trajectory of their adolescence.

As they approached Patience, she turned, and he saw

her profile in the full sunlight. She wore scrubs with a hoodie that had the K9 clinic logo emblazoned on the front. To the casual eye, or someone who didn't know her well, she might appear to have grown thicker around her middle. Not unheard-of as people hit thirty years old; Nash heard so many of the officers at the RRPD complain about having to cut back calories and increase their workouts to maintain professional standards in uniform. But Patience's belly was more pronounced today, and he couldn't keep the grin off his face. That was their babies growing inside her.

His breath whooshed out of his lungs as he saw how her eyes lit up when she recognized the boys, and then him. Knowing the swell of her belly was from their lovemaking added oxygen to the ferocious protective flames he'd felt since finding out she was pregnant.

"Nash, are you and Greta going to do agility or signals first?" Officer Juliette Walsh, who was dating Patience's brother, walked up and stood next to him, watching the scene unfold.

"I haven't decided. How about you?"

Juliette nodded at the beagle on her heels. "Sasha and I are going to work on signals today, aren't we, girl?" Sasha was a narcotics dog and her expert sniffer had kept a lot of illegal substances out of the hands of Red Ridge teens.

"Life will be better for all of us once we shut down the drug ring," Nash stated. Juliette knew as much as he did, and probably assumed the Larsons were responsible, but it wasn't their place to indict without evidence and a solid case. Most of that was left up to the RRPD detectives. K9 did the heavy lifting as far as drug detection and interdiction, as well as search and rescue to include diving.

"It sure will be. I'm sick of anyone around here thinking they can take advantage of the good people of this town." Juliette looked over at Patience, then back to him. "I hear you've been spending time with Blake's sister, Nash," she added with a smile.

"Greta and I were first on scene when she witnessed the Lake Killer dumping the victim, yes." He suspected Juliette wasn't referring to the Lake Killer case, though.

His colleague grinned. "I'm just busting on you. Blake's father couldn't wait to tell us he'd been to Patience's cabin, and that he'd run into you there."

Nash froze. Had Fenwick blabbed about the baby before he and Patience had had a chance to tell their relatives themselves?

"Before you get all upset, Patience let Blake know about my future niece and nephew—when Blake and I can finally marry, that is. He couldn't keep it to himself. I'm so excited for you both."

Nash smiled. "And count on me doing everything in my power to keep Patience and the babies safe through this case and beyond."

"I've got your back if you ever need it," Juliette said. "See you on the field. Come on, Sasha." They walked away and Nash took a few moments to calm down.

Patience needed him to be the calm and cool one, not a hothead. He saw the boys talking to her as they stood with Greta, Juliette and Sasha, and immediately relaxed. They were all family now, no matter what happened between him and Patience.

* * *

For the next few hours Patience helped out at the K9 training center, working with the handlers and trainers to put the dogs into every conceivable situation they'd face on the street. Drug and bomb detection, search and rescue, guarding. She got a kick out of watching Jon's and Troy's expressions when the usually laid-back Greta turned into a focused, take-no-prisoners attack dog and grabbed the heavily padded arm of one of the trainers.

"Are we going to do any water training today, Dr. Colton?" Jon Maddox's face resembled Nash's so much she wondered if either of the twins would look the same.

"No, Greta's had enough real time in the lake lately." With a chill that had nothing to do with the crisp autumn day, she realized Greta might have more diving to do if the Lake Killer came back. Looking past the fences, she wondered if the thug was out there, watching from a hidden location.

"Hey, what are you thinking?" Nash was next to her, close enough to touch her, but not doing so. He was professional if nothing else. But with the thought of such a bad guy being out there, she wanted to lean against Nash, let him take care of protecting her and the twins.

Where on earth had that come from? The baby hormones were making a mess of her self-reliance pact with herself.

"I'm thinking it's time to bring everyone in for the potluck lunch. Are your sisters coming to join us?"

"Not today. Paige has senior class activities and Maeve is with a study group. Which reminds me— I'm signed up to chaperone the senior Fall Fest dance. I was hoping you'd join me."

"Are you asking me out on a date?"

"I'd never do such a cheap date, if it was a date. This is a way to be able to keep an eye on you and also let you get to know my siblings. Meet them on their turf, so to speak."

"How are you going to explain my baby bump to the other PTA members?"

"Do you care?" His eyes blazed with molten heat and her body's immediate response made her sit down on a nearby bench. "Are you okay?" His lust turned to concern so quickly that Patience had to laugh.

"I'm good. Just adjusting to all the changes." She rubbed the tops of her thighs before pressing her hands into her lower back as she stretched her legs out in front. "I needed to get off my feet for a bit, that's all."

"I'm going to be by your side through all of this, babe."

"We'll talk about it later, Nash."

He said nothing. Patience would figure out he wasn't going anywhere. Nash just had to keep showing up.

Chapter 16

After the training center potluck, Nash left Greta with Patience for protection and took the boys home. He'd tried to convince himself that it'd be okay to bring Patience back to the house for dinner, but it would be a stupid move with the Lake Killer still at large. And now he had the Larsons' dog walker to worry about.

It was past dark when he drove up the mountain to the cabin. The only way to see was with the Jeep's brights on, given the tree branches reaching out from both sides of the asphalt. As he approached the turnoff to the graveled road that led to Patience's front gate, he was startled by a huge lumbering figure that came out to block the road.

Acting on pure instinct, he hit the brakes and the horn, staying focused on the figure as his vehicle came to a rough halt. It wasn't the Lake Killer or a Larson twin, though. A huge black bear stared him down from its stance in the center of his path, and he had the distinct impression it was sizing him up. It lifted its snout in the air as if it could tell who he was by his scent. Only then did Nash notice a smaller bear, about the size of Greta, meandering through the headlight beams. A mama bear with her cub, out for the last of the autumn feeding before they had to go into hibernation.

Nash took his hand from the wheel, no longer interested in honking. As he watched the scene play out, an unexpected rush of compassion rolled through him.

He loved his siblings and had accepted long ago that it was his role to help raise them. And he'd planned on years of bachelorhood, once the kids left for college and whatever their lives might bring. All this he expected and looked forward to. Discovering that he and Patience had created a baby had been a huge surprise, but to his shock, it wasn't a bad thing.

The mother bear and cub moved in unison, working their way across the road and back into the dark woods, as if he didn't exist. The natural beauty of it moved him.

As much as he had a family, raising his siblings, Nash wanted more. He wanted to feel so in tune with another that she'd know he'd always be there for her. And he loved the idea of waking up to a sensuous woman like Patience Colton every morning. And going to bed with her every night.

Nash wanted more than he'd ever thought he would.

As he put the car back in Drive, he realized that it wasn't what he wanted that mattered. This inexplicable emotion he had for Patience and their unborn children was his problem. His job was to be whatever Patience needed him to be. She'd made it clear that she valued her independence above all.

Patience wasn't much of a cook except when she came to the cabin, the one place she ever felt she truly had the time and space to prepare a proper meal. She took in the huge bowl of pasta carbonara she'd prepared, and while a nice glass of red wine would have been nice, it was easy to forgo for the health of the babies. Her stomach growled and she dug in.

As she twisted a second forkful of pasta, dripping with melted Parmesan, on her plate, Greta let out her warning barks. Patience paused midbite and looked at the monitor atop the island counter. Expecting to see Nash's Jeep, she felt her heart slam into overdrive when she saw an unfamiliar red pickup creep up the drive.

She dropped the fork and ran to the bedroom, where she retrieved her weapon from the safe. After making sure it was locked and loaded, she made her way back to the kitchen and turned out the lights. How had she gone from routine K9 surgeries to needing to draw her weapon multiple times in a few short weeks?

"Greta, here." She pointed to the floor behind the kitchen island to offer the dog the most protection. "Quiet."

Greta sat but remained alert, and Patience wished she could read her mind. Wished the dog could tell her what she smelled and what she heard.

The computer display lit up as the motion detector

light turned on, and she grabbed the monitor and put it on the floor next to her so that it wouldn't give the intruder a clue as to where she was, or if she was in the cabin. Her car was parked around back, so it wouldn't be obvious to anyone that she was home.

Unless this was Nash and he'd taken one of the RRPD pool vehicles. In which case she was going to berate him. Patience glued her gaze to the screen, and felt her stomach sink when she didn't recognize the person who got out of the vehicle. It was a male, over six feet tall, and he held a gun in his right hand. But it wasn't Nash. Patience immediately called 9-1-1.

"Nine-one-one. What's your emergency?" Frank's voice, sure and calm.

"Frank, it's Patience Colton. I'm in my cabin in the mountains and there is an intruder with a weapon, looks like a Colt .45, approaching my front door."

As she relayed the information, a gunshot cracked through the air, followed by loud pounding.

"He's breaking into my house!"

"Are you armed, Patience?"

"Yes." She braced her elbows on the island and aimed at the front door. The wood splintered and shuddered as it resisted the thug's attack, but within seconds the door burst open. The porch motion light backlit the man, and Patience thought she recognized his profile as that of the same suspect who'd been caught on security cameras at the clinic, running Nico and the puppy to a get-away car. One of the Larsons' henchmen. She watched him break into her home with a surreal detachment.

"Stop! I have a weapon."

Greta whimpered next to her, clearly wanting to break her silence and lunge for the intruder.

"You don't steal someone else's property and think you'll get away with it." Another gunshot rang out and granite exploded no more than a foot from her.

Patience was done with talking. She fired at the figure, aiming as she'd practiced countless times on the RRPD range and during the K9 exercises. It wasn't expected that as a veterinarian she'd ever have to fire a weapon, and it wasn't something she'd ever wanted to do until now.

The man jerked, and she wasn't sure if she'd hit his shoulder or his leg, but she saw his arms drop as he fell backward onto the porch. She took her flashlight and shone it at him. His weapon was a foot away, out of his hand. Patience couldn't send Greta to investigate, not yet, not while he could still be conscious and reach for that gun.

"What's going on, Patience?" Frank asked over the phone.

"I've shot the intruder. He's down, half in and half out of my cabin. I believe he's one of the Larsons' henchmen. We'll need an ambulance along with the RRPD."

"Both already on their way. Nash is almost there."

Nash had heard the call on his police radio, she was certain. He'd probably missed the shooter by minutes.

Dispatch must have heard the shots over the phone and sent the ambulance, per standard operating procedure.

Patience carefully crawled around the island and to the sofa on her belly. The bulge that felt like an eggplant was undeniable. The babies. She could not—would not—risk her children. She had to make sure this person was disarmed.

He groaned, his eyes closed. The gun was inches from his outstretched hand, near the back corner of the sofa, on the hardwood floor. She'd hurt him, but how badly was impossible to tell.

Two more feet and she'd be able to grab his weapon, then have Greta guard him until the EMTs and the RRPD arrived. She timed her movements with his groans, hoping to hide the sound of her crawling. Peering from behind the sofa, she ascertained that he had no other visible weapons. His left shoulder was soaked with blood, where she'd hit him.

Finally, she was only a few inches away, stretched out on her side with her gun ready to fire again. Her fingers stretched for his weapon—and his arm swung to hit hers.

"Greta!" Patience swiped his gun and sent it skittering across the hardwood as Greta bounded from the kitchen area, leaped over Patience and landed on the assailant's chest. The man cried out in pain and surprise. Greta stood her ground as trained, and Patience let out a quick sigh of relief. He wasn't going anywhere as long as Greta was on him.

She moved back to the kitchen and turned on the lights, just as a pair of headlights swept up to the porch. A door slammed and Greta let out her signature bark that was only for Nash. She'd done her job.

Nash's heart had been in his throat the entire time he'd raced up the mountain, fighting to get there before the Larsons' thug hurt Patience, all thoughts of the bears behind him. He'd known fear for his siblings when they'd initially struggled to regroup after their parents had been killed. The occasional case or law enforcement situation shook him up. But nothing came close to the abject terror that had clutched him the moment he'd heard the dispatch call in response to Patience's distress over the radio.

He'd also heard that she'd neutralized the killer, with some help from Greta. Thank God.

As he pulled up in the clearing, his terror returned in an icy wave at the sight of the downed criminal, Greta with two paws on the man's chest.

Nash got out of his Jeep and ran up to the porch.

"Good girl, Greta."

She didn't acknowledge him; she was in work mode and her job was to keep this loser pinned down. Nash recognized the man as a thug paid by the Larsons, but had to know Patience was okay. He searched the immediate vicinity for her and it was a full second before he met her gaze across the room. She stood in the kitchen, her hair in a disheveled ponytail, stomach bulging under her tight white T-shirt. The babies. She and the twins were okay. It was all that mattered.

"You all right?"

Patience nodded, and offered him a shaky smile. "We're good. Just keep him away from me, okay?"

His pleasure.

"What the hell did you think you were doing?"

This particular henchman had done the Larsons' dirty work for a long time. He had a rap sheet a mile long. Problem was he was sneaky and wily, and for years had eluded conviction for the many felonies he was suspected of committing. Not any longer.

"Screw you." Even in his pain and with a pretty nasty gunshot wound, the criminal was still a jerk. A jerk who could have killed Patience and the babies. Pure unadulterated rage hit Nash sideways. It was primal.

"Nash." Patience's voice reached him and he forced the emotions into the compartmentalized box they had to go in, until he could examine them later. Right now he had to focus on getting the intruder the medical care he obviously needed and arresting him.

Sirens pierced the stillness of the mountain forest and an RRPD unit, followed by one of the Red Ridge hospital ambulances, pulled up next to his Jeep.

Juliette Walsh and her K9 partner, Sasha, ran up to the porch and nodded at Nash. "Patience okay?"

"She's fine—see for yourself."

"I'll take your word for it." Juliette took over the scene, directing the EMTs and two other RRPD officers she'd brought with her. Within twenty minutes the thug was on a stretcher and en route to Red Ridge Hospital. Under RRPD escort, of course.

Patience had never seen this side of Nash before. Outwardly, he appeared himself, an even more content version of the Nash who routinely juggled four kids, a law enforcement career and K9 handling protocol. It was the tightness in his throat muscles and the way he kept clenching and unclenching his fists that clued her in.

As soon as all the first responders had left, Patience pulled out duct tape and large plastic leaf bags. "Here, help me patch up the doorway. We're going to have to make do with it tonight. I'll call in a repair on it tomorrow."

"I'll make the repair tomorrow. We don't want any strangers here."

"Larson already found me." She paused and looked at Nash. "And I heard that there have been sightings of the Lake Killer in the eastern part of the state. It doesn't sound like he's looking for me anymore."

"We thought we'd taken care of the Larson twins and the dogs when we sent them running from the clinic. That didn't work out so well." Nash peeled out a length of tape and ripped it with his teeth.

"Here." She handed him a box cutter. "It's easier on your teeth."

He grimaced.

"Wait, Nash—stop." She placed her hand on his arm. "What's going on with you?"

For a moment she thought he was going to just ignore her, keep adding tape to the tarp-like contraption the front door was becoming. Finally, he lowered his arms and looked at her.

"I wasn't here for you. Before you tell me that it's okay, don't. I know it's impossible for me to be everywhere, and you and our children are going to face dangerous situations that neither of us see coming. Not so insane as this—" he waved at the door "—but life isn't safe, not all the time. I'm a cop. I know this."

"If you're not beating yourself up about not getting here before I had to shoot him, what is it, then?"

"It hadn't hit me yet just how much responsibility a family is. That sounds stupid coming from me, right? I worry about my siblings all the time. Are they getting enough affection? Am I listening to them? Do they feel they can come to me about anything from drugs to sex? Have I handled the girls okay? You know, the female necessities—periods, gynecological health, how to handle boys who are rude to them. Will I be able to be enough of a father figure for the boys?" He paused, his hands on his hips, his face down. When he looked up at her again his eyes glittered with angst. "No matter what, I know that whatever I can do for the kids is good—it's better than what they'd have without me. These babies, our children, it's different. It is totally my responsibility how they turn out."

"Hey, come here." She tugged his arm until he shifted, and she led him to the sofa.

"I don't want to sit down, Patience. I need to move."

"You can move all you want in a minute. Let me have my say."

He complied, but his face was screwed up in an expression of pain that told her she had only a few minutes to talk to him.

"First, you don't have to worry about the babies if you don't want to. I've already told you that I don't expect anything from you. Not in a hard or mean way, but in a real, I-can-handle-this-myself way." She ignored the tug at her conscience. Yes, she'd appreciated him being near and protecting her. More than she'd ever imagined. But she didn't need him to keep her safe. Hadn't she just proved that?

"Second, you're doing a great job with your siblings, by all accounts. Word gets around the RRPD and I've never heard anyone say anything other than very complimentary words about how your siblings behave. You're raising fine kids, Nash. Which brings me to three."

He grunted and she couldn't help but laugh.

"You're going to be a wonderful father. I get that you are the forever bachelor, and trust me, I'm not looking for anything permanent with a man." *Liar.* She hadn't been, but being with Nash all these hours and days had added up. Her heart was getting too used to him. "But we've created these babies together, and I think between the two of us we'll work it out. Lots of people co-parent."

"Are you done?"

She let out a sigh. "Yes."

He got on his knees in front of her and cupped her face with his hands. "I never want to feel the terror I did driving up this mountain again. Ever. I thought… I thought I'd lost you, Patience." Nash didn't finesse his move; he crushed his mouth to hers.

Patience kissed him back, hoping her lips conveyed her belief in him.

But it wasn't Nash she was worried about. Tonight's intruder was tame compared to what still lurked out there. The Lake Killer. She knew he'd never give up until she was dead.

Chapter 17

Nash mentally fought against leaving Patience the next day. His only conciliation was that they'd made love until midnight, after which he'd been able to hold her through the predawn hours.

He leaned back in his desk chair at work and appreciated the creaking that usually annoyed him. It grounded his spirit, reminded him that nothing had hurt Patience or the babies last night.

They'd agreed to table the discussion on what they were going to do about their relationship, at least until the Lake Killer was captured. As single parents, working as a parenting team, or as more. The "more" part had him stymied.

He was afraid to approach Patience with what he wanted, what he thought might be best. She should move in with him and the kids. It made the most sense. His house was equipped for a family, and would easily incorporate the twins.

"Maddox, I need to you go over to Hamlin Harrington's house with Officer Walsh." Chief Finn Colton stood over him. Jeez, he hadn't even heard his boss approach. Nash stood.

"Yes, sir."

"Hamlin says he caught Demi Colton red-handed after she broke into his house. She took off before he could catch her."

"'Catch her'?"

"Yeah, I feel the same as you. It's a good thing that woman can run. If she was indeed the person who was there. He's positive she'll show up on his security camera's footage, so head on out there and find out what you can."

"Sir, I understand that catching the Groom Killer is our top priority, but I'm working the Lake Killer case at the moment." He never questioned an order, but there was no way he'd take his focus off the Lake Killer case unless absolutely necessary. Although he couldn't defend his motives fully, not until Finn knew that Patience carried Nash's kids.

"I know you're providing protection for Patience, and that's a standing requirement of the Lake Killer case. But our good K9 vet is safe at the clinic and I'm shorthanded. I need to you to interview Hamlin, and then corroborate it with a statement from his son, Devlin."

Finn must have seen the stress on his face and interpreted it as friendly concern for Patience. Not too long ago Nash would have had no problem convincing himself the same. But after making love to her with such frequency and need over the past weeks, seeing those two babies on the ultrasound screen, hearing their heartbeats, Nash knew he couldn't dismiss his bond with Patience as merely friendly.

But what was it?

"Devlin's easy enough to pin down," Nash said. Harrington's billionaire status meant all of Red Ridge knew his family, too. His son, Devlin, ran his portion of the business in town. "I can catch up with him in his office."

"I knew I could count on you, Nash. If you need to break away to help Patience or the other case, do so."

"I'm on it, Chief."

"You and Juliette be careful out there, Nash. There's no telling what that man is thinking half the time. And we need to find out what Demi's looking for. Why would she risk her life to break into Harrington's mansion? It's practically a fortress." The chief shook his head. "He's convinced she was trying to kill him."

Nash knew this couldn't be easy on the chief; Demi was his cousin. But Finn Colton was always professional.

"Hamlin Harrington's always been a little off-kilter." He didn't want to come right out and say he thought the dude lived in a bubble that a lot of money bought.

"That's not our job, Nash." The chief didn't argue with his assessment of the senior Harrington, though. The RRPD received its share of house calls out to his home. Harrington seemed haunted by the possibility of being kidnapped or killed for his fortune.

"Got it, Chief." When his boss left, Nash signaled to Greta. She stood up from her resting spot and came to his side.

"You're ready to work again, aren't you, partner?"

Her large Newfie tail thumped in agreement.

Patience pulled into the K9 clinic parking lot and saw no handlers or dogs in the training center's large fenced area. There hadn't been more training scheduled for her since Saturday, a good thing, meaning all injured K9s were back on duty.

She grabbed the caramel decaf latte she'd bought for herself and the dozen doughnuts for the training center and clinic staff. After the shock of the attempted break-in, plus absorbing the fact she was having not one but two babies, she'd needed something fun to distract herself. Treating the employees to a sweet seemed to be the perfect choice.

Balancing her bag, coffee and doughnuts, she closed the car door with her hip.

"Patience."

The female voice came out of nowhere and startled her. She turned on her heel to face a woman dressed entirely in black, with a hooded jacket. Only after she pushed back her hood did Patience identify her.

"Demi!" Her cousin, wanted for questioning in relation to the murders of several would-have-been grooms in the Red Ridge area, stood in front of her.

Demi didn't look like a killer. Her pallor and shadowed

eyes reflected the burden of accusation without evidence, the constant stress of life on the run.

"Patience. I'm sorry, I didn't mean to frighten you. It seems I have this effect on people lately."

Patience put the box, purse and coffee on the hood of her car. "I'm not afraid of you, Demi. I know you better than most, and I've never thought of you as anything but a sweet person." They hadn't grown up together, since they came from opposite ends of town and the Colton family tree. But she would never forget how Demi had brought in that injured stray dog right before she'd fled. In Patience's mind, a woman capable of cold-blooded murder wouldn't be so concerned about a poor animal.

A ghost of a smile crossed Demi's pretty features. "The rest of Red Ridge doesn't agree with you."

"Who cares?" As Patience spoke, her gaze caught on Demi's black sweatshirt. A bounty hunter, Demi never appeared anything less than fully capable of the athletic feats her work often required of her. Fugitives weren't always the acquiescent type. Demi's stomach protruded under her zippered hoodie as if she'd been indulging in the doughnuts on the car hood. But her bump moved.

"Before you ask, yes, this is my baby." Demi hadn't missed Patience's observation. She turned and unzipped her jacket far enough that Patience could see the tiny face. The baby was cocooned in a sling up against her mom, covered by the jacket.

"How old?"

Demi stood up straight. "Four months. Don't ask me more—I'm not going to tell you."

Patience studied the baby. Demi had been jilted by

Bo Gage right after they'd gotten engaged. He'd dumped her for Hayley Patton, a not-so-nice local girl. It must have been humiliating for Demi. But no way had she killed Bo or the other victims, as many accused her of doing. "You know I don't think you're the Groom Killer, Demi."

"Yet you don't know, do you? I certainly have motive. First, I'm left practically at the altar, then my ex-fiancé shows up dead. What I want to know is why no one's looking at other potential suspects."

"I'm sure the RRPD is looking at a lot of people. But it's not that simple. You've heard about the murder here—" she motioned toward the lake "—about a month ago?"

Demi nodded. "Yes. I heard that you're the only witness."

"Word sure gets around in Red Ridge." She didn't confirm or deny Demi's comment. "You know you're wanted for questioning, right?" Patience didn't have authority to arrest or even compel Demi to report to the police. But she hated seeing her cousin, a new mother, so torn up, obviously being accused of something she hadn't done.

Demi nodded. "I know. If you need to call the police on me, go ahead. To be honest, the running gets old. But I have to gather information no one else is willing to."

"What do you mean?"

She held up her hand. "Sorry. I'm thinking out loud. I came by for two reasons. First, to see how the dog that I brought by is."

"He's fine. He made it and was placed with a family

soon after you dropped him off. That was a kind thing you did, Demi."

"My other motive for seeking you out is that I need you to tell your father to back off. I'm not the Groom Killer, and by funneling everyone's attention on me he's keeping us all from finding the real murderer. That's why I'm so reluctant to walk into the RRPD on my own. Chances of me being held are high, with the town gossip stirred up and your father's pull. I don't want to be apart from my baby."

Patience couldn't argue with her, on any of it. Fenwick used his weight as mayor to influence everything from the usual local politics to business deals. He saw no shame in playing judge and jury when the town was in such an uproar. There'd been no official weddings in Red Ridge since the Groom Killer struck. It was bad for local business, especially the bakery, florists and dress designers. But more, it damaged morale. Fenwick Colton counted on a happy town to be reelected.

"My daddy might only have his mayor position when it all is said and done. His energy business is floundering."

"Yeah, that's been going on for a good while now. Hamlin Harrington hasn't helped—he's done everything to undermine your father's corporation."

"Why do you say that?"

"Doesn't Layla fill you in? Colton Energy has been bleeding funds for over two years. Harrington was helping that, in the hopes he'd be able to buy the entire company out. Looks like it's going to happen, from what I read on the stock pages. My research into trying to clear my name has brought me down some interesting roads."

An icy chill ran across Patience's skin. She'd been overwhelmed by her own pregnancy and so busy since the Lake Killer that she'd not seen the writing on the ledger books. Her sister was planning to marry a very bad man.

"Thanks for sharing that with me, Demi. I don't suppose you want to come inside, get warm, have a cup of coffee?"

Demi shook her head decisively. "No, not possible, I'm afraid. I'll take a rain check, though. For sooner than later, if the RRPD figures out who the real killer is."

"I have faith that they will."

"I hope you're right." She turned to leave, then paused. "I'm okay, Patience. I have a solid place to live, and I'm keeping myself and my baby safe. It's what matters right now. Being a mother has taught me to value the most basic necessities."

"I understand." And she did, much more than Demi realized.

Her cousin's assessment of her form was quick, exacting. "I see that you do. How far along are you?"

Her hand instinctively went to her midsection. "Four months."

"You're slimmer than me, usually. Are you sure you're only four months along?"

Patience nodded. She didn't want to tell Demi it was twins.

"Well, congrats to you, too."

"If you need anything, Demi—"

"I know I can contact you, thanks. That's what I'm doing now. Please talk to your father for me. The resolution of the Groom Killer case depends upon it."

"I will."

Demi put her hood back on, ducked her head and hurried to a nondescript dark, beat-up truck. Patience was torn—she worked for the county and her clinic served the RRPD. No doubt many would say she should immediately call in Demi's location. But she trusted her gut, which told her her cousin wasn't the Groom Killer. But with all the evidence pointing that way, if Demi was innocent, then who was the Groom Killer?

Just as she'd witnessed the Lake Killer dumping a body, certainly someone in all of Red Ridge must have witnessed the Groom Killer in one capacity or another. The murders hadn't happened in a vacuum.

She looked at her latte, now cold, and the box of doughnuts on the hood of her car. It wouldn't make a difference if she delayed going into the clinic long enough to make a phone call. She pulled out her cell and hit the speed dial for Nash. He'd know what to do.

And she trusted him implicitly.

Chapter 18

"I'm telling you both, Demi Colton stood right where you two are with a gun in her hand, ready to kill me." Hamlin Harrington spoke to Nash and Juliette, the massive river-stone fireplace in his great room a backdrop to his dramatic retelling of Demi's break-in.

"We aren't doubting how you felt, Mr. Harrington." Juliette spoke up as Nash took Greta around the room, sniffing for anything unusual. The security camera revealed that Demi had indeed entered the mansion via a back sliding door. But unlike how Harrington described it, she hadn't broken any glass or picked a lock—she'd opened an unlocked door.

"Then why do I get the impression that none of you at the Red Ridge Police Department are taking me seriously?" Harrington's face reddened, which Nash would have thought impossible on his perpetually ruddy skin.

"Of course, we're taking you seriously, Mr. Harrington. It's why Officer Walsh and I came out as soon as we could, and why Sasha and Greta are with us. We aren't going to miss a thing with their noses, trust me."

"What is she sniffing for, exactly?" Harrington wanted to channel his anger onto someone, and his annoyed expression focused on Greta.

Nash fought back a sarcastic response. Hamlin Harrington was a man of means who didn't take "no" for an answer, but Nash would be damned if he'd let the man take aim at his K9. At the end of the day, Harrington was a civilian and had no jurisdiction over the RRPD or its K9 officers.

"Come, Greta."

The dog trotted to his side and sat.

"Greta's been looking for any signs of drugs or other illegal substances that the intruder may have left behind."

"You mean like explosives?"

"Among many other things."

"It wouldn't surprise me that a woman like that brought in a lot of illegal substances with her."

"Well, our K9 doesn't agree with you. There's no sign of anything other than what you've shared and what your security footage reveals. Demi Colton was here, but she left without harming you or apparently taking anything. You're certain nothing is missing?"

"No, I'm not certain. Have a look at this place, will you? It'll take me a few days to figure out what she took." Harrington waved his arms at the heavily decorated interior, chock-full of what were probably expensive paintings and sculptures. Nash wasn't into art, and had no idea what the various pieces were worth. He looked at Juliette, in an easy stance by Harrington's massive carved desk. The piece of furniture clearly came from another century, but the state-of-the-art computer and monitor atop it showed it had plenty of twenty-first-century use. Whatever Demi had come in here for, she'd either gotten it before Harrington intercepted her or she'd given up before she bolted. Nash doubted she had tried to harm Harrington. So far, every time the woman showed up anywhere she hadn't hurt anyone. The town chatter pointed toward her as the Groom Killer, but absolutely no evidence did.

And there was Patience's opinion to consider. Demi was her cousin, and while the two weren't close, it was clear that Patience trusted her. Patience made it clear that she thought Demi an innocent victim of town gossip.

"We'll take a few last photographs before we leave, if that's okay with you, sir." Juliette played the good cop very well, and Nash swallowed a snicker. He and Juliette had plenty to discuss on the ride back into town.

"You don't think Demi's guilty, do you?" Juliette spoke from the passenger seat as Nash drove them back to the station. She had another case to work and Nash could handle Devlin Harrington on his own. Nash hated that he wasn't the one splitting off and heading to the K9 clinic. To Patience.

"Honestly, no, I don't. But I'm not a detective and we don't have all the facts yet. It would make things a lot less complicated if we were able to question her."

"We have to find her first."

Nash let out a long sigh. "Yeah, I know. And we will. She's right here in town." He frowned. "What's with Red Ridge lately? Everything is being turned upside down. Our quiet part of paradise is definitely on troubled waters."

"We've got two killers on the loose, maybe more if one or both of them are part of a larger crime ring. It's daunting." Juliette stared out the windshield and Nash thought she looked as frustrated as he felt.

"But not impossible to solve." Nash valued looking at the big picture, then narrowing down to specifics. "Let's pull ourselves up to an eagle-eye view. Hamlin Harrington is involved in what local business at the moment?"

"He wants to bail out Fenwick Colton. Harrington's a corporate shark. He smells the blood of failing industry, and to him, it's opportunity."

"Right. But why? What's in it for him?"

"Interest back on the money he lent."

"What else?" Nash knew there had to be more.

"Power, I'd imagine. Men like Harrington love holding the keys to the kingdom, so to speak. Nowadays, if you're in control of a population's energy source, that's the epitome of power, don't you think?"

"I suppose." Nash pulled into the RRPD's lot. "Here you go. Nice work this morning."

"We all work well together, that's certain." Juliette got out of the car and let her K9 out of the back.

As he watched the two of them walk into the station, Nash's phone rang. Patience. If he were a sentimental man he'd swear little cartoon hearts like the ones in the quirky cartoons the boys watched burst from the phone.

"Hey, babe."

"Nash, this isn't a personal call. I just spoke to Demi Colton."

Nash's stomach twisted, no matter his thoughts on Demi's innocence. The safety of Patience and the babies was everything to him. "Where? Are you okay?"

"Of course I'm fine. I had just pulled into the clinic and she walked up to my car. You know I trust her. She's my cousin, and besides, she's not the Groom Killer, Nash. No way do I believe it. No matter what my father and the rest of Red Ridge think."

"What did she want?"

"She wants me to tell my father to back off, for one."

"That's fair, if she isn't guilty."

"Then why do you sound so disappointed?" Patience knew him better than he knew himself. It should frighten him, the way their bond exponentially grew, but instead he liked the warmth it shot through his chest.

"Because she needs to come in for questioning. It'd be best if I could get a statement from her, once and for all. Is she still there? On clinic property?"

"No, she left after only a few minutes. To be honest, Nash, if I were her I'm not certain I'd trust the RRPD right now."

"Excuse me? You're as much a part of the police force as I am, Patience."

"Sure, but you're not understanding what I'm saying. If I were Demi and the entire town was convinced I'd killed someone, even though I'm innocent, I wouldn't risk being taken into custody. Especially because…"

"Because?"

"She had a baby with her, Nash."

He immediately recalled the security footage from Harrington's house. "Then why would she risk going to Harrington's?" It didn't make sense to him.

"She's trying to figure out who the Groom Killer is, too, Nash. Because it's not her."

"I want to agree with you, Patience, but I have to follow this through to the end. We need all the facts." He told her what he'd been assigned to do. "I'm on my way to interview Devlin Harrington now. Don't worry, I'll be back at the cabin with you tonight."

She laughed. "That's the least of my worries. I can't stay up all night like we've been doing—I'm useless at work this tired."

"There's a big difference between 'tired' and 're-laxed.'" His teasing drew another laugh from her and he enjoyed the ring of her giggles over the connection. A small moment in the midst of a large, grim case, but it made him smile, too. With a jolt he saw that this bond with Patience wasn't just about the huge aspect of becoming parents together, or the danger of facing the Lake Killer, but more. As in he'd never felt like this about another woman.

"Yes, well, you've got me feeling both today, Nash."

"I'll see you later, babe." He disconnected and allowed himself to daydream about Patience's eyes as he drove downtown.

"Be a good dog, Greta, and have a nap."

Harrington, Inc. occupied an old bank building on Main Street that had been refurbished into office spaces. Nash decided to leave Greta in the back of the SUV, not wanting to be turned away by anyone at the swanky business.

Devlin ran the IT branch of the company for his father, but from what Nash knew, the oily son of a billionaire pretty much did whatever the heck he wanted. Devlin had a reputation in town as too slick for his abilities, and Nash had come face-to-face with Devlin's smarmy side personally when they'd played in a town softball tournament to raise funds for the K9 clinic. Devlin didn't know a softball mitt from a gardener's glove, yet he'd paraded all over the diamond as if he played in the major leagues. Nash wasn't in the mood for more of the same this afternoon. Not with two killers loose in Red Ridge, one directly targeting the woman he—

No, he wasn't going there. The mother of his unborn children was at risk, and the Lake Killer case needed closure. This sidetrack to cover some of the investigative work for the Groom Killer case had to be done, and Nash had no problem doing it. As long as he held Patience in his arms tonight.

"Good afternoon, Patti." He flashed a wide smiled

at the receptionist, a high school classmate he'd run alongside on the cross-country team.

"Nash Maddox! I haven't seen you in a while. I'll bet you're busy with the Groom Killer case, aren't you?"

"We all are. How's your family?" He wasn't afraid to use their personal connection and some good old-fashioned manners to get what he wanted.

After they caught one another up on their lives, he leaned in for the kill. "I'm here to talk to Devlin. Is he in?"

"He sure is." Patti didn't pretend her boss wasn't available, to his relief. "Four doors down the hallway, on the right."

"Thanks a lot, Patti."

"Anytime."

Nash walked along the corridor and took in the cushy surroundings, the open office doors, their occupants appearing hard at work as they sat or stood at computer desks. It was eerily quiet with no piped-in music since the workers he saw wore earbuds or headphones. He supposed it made sense. Still, it was damned creepy to have so many people working in a set space with little or no ambient noise. *Snap out of it.*

No matter how much he clung to police procedure, though, nothing could shake the sense of urgency he had to get to the bottom of both the Groom and Lake murders. Since the Lake Killer case came home to roost in his personal world, he'd been unable to shake a sense of foreboding.

Devlin's nameplate was on the wall next to his open door, and he stood with his back to the entrance. Nash took advantage of the opportunity to observe. Devlin looked at one of several computer monitors on his L-shaped desk. An open laptop displayed a familiar face that took Nash a mere heartbeat to recognize. Hayley Patton—the woman the first victim of the Groom Killer, Bo Gage, had been engaged to after Bo had dumped Demi Colton. Even if he didn't know Hayley from her connection to the murder victim, Nash knew her well because she was an excellent K9 trainer and he frequently worked with her at the center. Why would Devlin have Hayley Patton's picture on his laptop? Was it his screen saver? And again, why?

Nash rapped his knuckles on the doorjamb. Devlin turned on a dime and visibly blanched when he recognized him.

"Nash. What brings you into Harrington, Inc.?" Typical Devlin, invoking his billionaire family name by way of introduction. Very unlike Devlin, however, was how he jerkily slapped his laptop shut, making Hayley Patton's face disappear.

"I have some questions I need to ask you." He stepped into the office and watched as Devlin smoothed his hand over his shaved head with shaking hands. Odd. Devlin usually was the epitome of polished, to the point of creepy and oily.

"Have a seat." Devlin sank into his chair before Nash sat down. He'd definitely spooked the man and it had something to do with Hayley Patton. He made a mental note to see if there was a connection between Devlin and Hayley in Bo Gage's murder file.

"Thanks. I won't take too much of your time, but as you probably know, your father had a break-in at his home. According to him, Demi Colton broke into the house and threatened to kill him." He deliberately left out the part about Demi sliding open an unlocked door.

"Yes, my father told me. Have you or any of your colleagues apprehended her yet?" Accusation blazed in Devlin's beady eyes. The man's recovery from being caught with the image of a murder victim's fiancée on his laptop stunned even Nash. He'd witnessed plenty of human behavior over the years. Just because Devlin annoyed the heck out of him and most of Red Ridge, it didn't mean the man was a criminal.

It didn't mean he wasn't, either.

"We're exploring every aspect of the case at hand. To the best of your knowledge, does your dad have anything of interest to Demi Colton?"

Devlin smirked with his signature lip curl. "What doesn't he have is more like it. That b—woman's from the other side of town. I don't have to tell you that. And the entire Colton family seems to be after my father to bail them out. Some do legally, like Fenwick Colton. Others, not so much. Demi wanted drug money, I'd guess. When she didn't find loose cash, she was going to steal a painting. My father has a lot of valuable artwork."

Nash stared at Devlin, hard. "What makes you think she was attempting to steal any of your father's art?" Hamlin had said nothing marginally close to this, and the security footage only showed Demi rifling through Hamlin's desk, his home office, attempting to get into his computer. She'd been looking for something, all right, but Nash's law enforcement instinct told him it was information. Not cash or artwork. Red Ridge was a large enough town at thirty-five thousand, but not big enough for a drug addict to hope to turn around a valuable for cash quick enough to get a fix.

Besides, Demi Colton had no record or history of drug use. And she had a baby to worry about. That could be enough motive for the money part, to feed her child. But why risk going to Harrington's?

"Please, Nash, spare me the interrogation technique. Demi Colton is at the very least a burglar, and at most..." He theatrically trailed off and Nash bit back his own snarl.

"At most?"

"Come on, Nash. I'm in IT and even I can see the trail. All you have to do is read the *Red Ridge Reporter* twice a week. Demi Colton is the one consistent thing, the common denominator, in all the Groom Killer murders. And she was dumped by Bo Gage—isn't that motive enough?"

"How do you know Hayley Patton, Devlin?"

Devlin's eyes narrowed, a remarkable feat considering how beady they were. "The detective sees a photo and thinks he's onto something."

"I'm not a detective, Devlin. Just a cop closing the loop on an intruder report. Answer my question."

"Hayley and I went to school together. We were classmates, I'm sure you know. Two classes behind you. She sent me her photo to airbrush—she wanted her professional head shot freshened up. She said she was applying for a new job. We have a couple of experts in digital imaging and I'm going to have one of them do it. I just haven't gotten around to it yet, which is why I have her photo downloaded on my laptop, as a constant reminder. I tend to get distracted with running our IT department."

Nice catch, liar. Devlin's statement needed to be corroborated with Hayley, and Nash hoped it was another officer who'd have the honor. He wanted to get back to Patience, ASAP.

Nash nodded. "Any other reason you can think of why Demi would break into your father's home?"

Devlin's chest flattened. He'd obviously expected Nash to continue on the Hayley questioning. Nash wondered if Finn had anyone keeping tabs on Devlin. He would after Nash told him what he'd witnessed.

"I told you what I think. She's a druggie looking for a fix. If my father hadn't caught her red-handed, she'd have searched the medicine cabinet for painkillers."

"You mean opioids?"

"Yes, whatever. Does it matter? You know something, Nash? I resent that my father is the victim of what could have escalated to a heinous crime, and yet you're sitting here all smug and official, giving *me* the third degree."

"I'm so sorry you feel like that, Devlin. This is a standard line of questioning used for similar situations. We're trying to figure out why Demi Colton broke into your father's home, as you said."

"'As I said'? She broke in—it's on the video!" Devlin's tanning-salon skin color took on a ruddy hue.

Nash stood. "Thanks for your time, Devlin. If you

think of anything else, give me a call." He placed his business card on the glass-topped desk.

Devlin remained in his seat. "What I need, what Red Ridge needs, is for the police to get to the bottom of all of this and put it to rest. The sooner Demi Colton's in custody, the sooner I know I'll sleep better."

Nash mentally counted to five; Devlin wasn't worth ten. He leaned over the desk, just far enough to make Devlin tip back in his chair.

"It seems to me that your specialty is being your daddy's lackey, and what did you say you do? IT. It's wise to not accuse anyone unless you have the full facts of the case to back up your claims. In fact, it's defamation of character."

Devlin snarled. "A loser like Demi Colton wouldn't know what that means, much less would she ever come after me or anyone else in town for it. But okay, I get it. You want to do your job, show that our tax dollars are being put to work, go ahead."

Nash straightened, never breaking eye contact. Devlin's gaze slid away, his faux in-control corporate mask back in place. But not before Nash saw the flash of naked terror in the man's eyes. Devlin Harrington hid something behind his snarky exterior, and Nash couldn't wait for the RRPD to figure out what it was.

"Thanks for your time." He left, feeling Devlin's eyes drilling into the back of his skull. As if he hated him.

Not something Nash would expect from just a slimy businessman.

Chapter 19

Later that day, Patience had finished with her routine vet checks. All the patients were doing well. A text from Nash indicated he wouldn't be able to break away from the casework Finn had assigned him until well after dinner. He didn't want her driving back to the cabin alone and she didn't argue. They'd drive together when he got off work, and she'd stay at the clinic under extra security until then. Except she wanted to go out for dinner.

Her stomach grumbled at the same time she felt a definite flutter in her belly. Patience laughed, unable to keep the joy from infusing her entire being. She called Layla from her office and was relieved to hear she could meet her for dinner at their favorite restaurant downtown. A couple hours with her sister would cure what ailed her—mental exhaustion from the case.

"Downtown" for Red Ridge meant Main Street, where several eating establishments were clustered. She and Layla met at the Rodeo Table, where Tex-Mex and Southwestern cuisine dominated the menu.

They each ordered fajitas—Patience, shrimp, and Layla, chicken—along with a side of guacamole to share.

Once they had the restaurant's signature *pico de gallo* salsa in front of them, Patience's news burst out of her mouth.

"I'm having twins." She watched Layla's face as she broke the news, and to her delight, sheer joy sparkled in her sister's smile.

"Patience, I'm so happy for you!" Layla leaned over the table and hugged her tightly, her sincerity evident.

"Thanks."

"I'm so excited. Twins!" Layla sat back down in the booth. "Have you told Daddy yet?"

"He knows I'm pregnant—he saw the pile of baby stuff Nash brought to the cabin. He wasn't so thrilled, to be honest."

"Daddy's a man who only has so much to give. And he's got a lot on his mind lately."

"The business still in free fall?"

Layla nodded. "Yes. But it's okay." She squared her shoulders. "Hamlin's going to bail us out." She didn't seem as confident about her fiancé as she had weeks ago. Or when she and Patience had exchanged ugly words about her engagement. The day before the night Patience lost herself in Nash's arms for the first time. When the twins were conceived.

"Layla, I haven't brought it up again because we got so mad at one another the last time we talked about your engagement. But really, honey, Hamlin Harrington? You're young, beautiful and kind. He's none of the above."

"But he has the means to save Colton Energy, which means your K9 clinic and training center will keep operating."

"You don't have to remind me of that."

"You know there are plenty of other ways we can keep the center up and running. The RRPD already has three grants they've applied for, and a couple of other private donors."

"That defeats the original pledge Daddy made to the center, for your mother." Layla spoke with a shadow of her usual feisty spirit. Maybe she'd finally begun to the see the light, and it wasn't Hamlin Harrington.

"The center is dedicated to my mother. That will never change." And if her mom was still alive and able to see how Fenwick operated these days, all about his business, to the exclusion of his family, Patience knew she'd not give a fig where the money came from, as long as the donor was legit.

Unlike Hamlin, who had his fingers in so many pots it was impossible to tell which of his business dealings were legit or not.

"Daddy wants to be the one to always fund the K9 center."

"That's a noble thought, but if the money's from Hamlin, it's not Daddy's, is it?"

Layla frowned. The expression crumpled her pretty

face and for the first time Patience noticed tiny lines on her sister's skin.

"You okay, Layla? All of the financial stress has to be getting to you."

She rubbed her temples, eyes closed. "I'm fine. And I'm not about to admit to you that marrying Hamlin wasn't my idea at all. I mean, in the long run, Daddy is looking out for all of us, right? And plenty of people get married for sheer convenience."

"Give me a break, Layla. Listen to yourself. You're selling yourself out, like a slave or a prostitute. Unless… did Hamlin agree to a platonic marriage?"

She shook her head. "No, he hasn't. We haven't… you know, done much, and I don't think there'd be a lot in that department after we're married. He's in his midseventies."

"Do I have to remind you of basic biology, dear sister? Or tell you about Viagra? If you don't want to have sex with Hamlin now, nothing will change after the vows. Stop letting Daddy use you like this!"

Layla's eyes filled with tears, but while Patience ached for her sister's struggle, she wasn't backing down.

"See this?" She grabbed a white napkin from the table and waved it like a banner. "It's my BS flag and I'm throwing it on your belief. Daddy isn't going to accept you or outwardly love you any more or less because you go along with one of his dirty financial schemes. He doesn't have it to give, Layla. You could sell your firstborn to appease him and he'd still be Daddy."

Layla sniffed, took a sip of her iced tea. "You're right. Of course. It's just that…"

"What is it, Layla? Underneath your need for Daddy's approval?"

Layla looked at her with huge eyes and Patience picked up on her half sister's sorrow. "What will happen to me if Daddy's business goes belly-up? I'm not like you, with a skill I can take anywhere. All I know how to do is follow Daddy around and clean up his financial messes."

"Are you kidding me? That's a huge gift. Not everyone can take the tangle he makes of things and unknot it, transforming it into something useful. You've singlehandedly turned around dozens of his damaging business deals, and kept the loan sharks from eating away at his earnings."

"I haven't done a good enough job or Hamlin wouldn't be my future husband."

Finally, Layla admitted her motive for marrying Harrington: she blamed herself for the problems at Colton Energy. Patience had felt that, but for Layla to voice it was huge.

She reached across the table and grasped Layla's hand. "Honey, you're doing a wonderful job for Daddy. But you have to do it for yourself first. Trust me, I learned that the hard way when I went off to college."

"And vet school." Layla wiped her eyes and managed a laugh. "I thought Daddy's head was going to explode when you refused all that money he offered you, wanting you to stay in Red Ridge and work for him."

Patience smiled at the memory. "He's never understood me, has he? All I've ever wanted to do, I'm doing. Work with animals and serve the community. Win-win."

"Daddy's all about the power. Yet underneath it, I have to believe he has a heart or else he wouldn't have endowed the clinic in your mama's name."

"No, he wouldn't have. But he's run out of funds, from all accounts. Care to comment?" Patience didn't expect Layla to divulge corporate secrets, but Fenwick had named all his children as heirs to his fortune. Which at the moment was at risk.

"If you're asking about your inheritance, don't worry. He put a good chunk of his wealth away for safekeeping. As for Colton Energy, yeah, he's in a boatload of trouble. Hamlin's not his only lifeline, you know. He's calling in favors and IOUs left and right."

"But it's not enough?"

Layla took a bite of fajita and chewed, obviously stalling. "We'll see." She poked at her food with her fork. "What about you, Patience? I know you're happy about the babies, but something's bugging you."

"Since witnessing the murder at the lake, I've been jumpy. That's all."

"And they still haven't caught the creep?"

"No." She didn't want to tell Layla how much the Lake Killer had affected her. No need to burden her sister with her concerns.

"I worry about you. I'm glad Nash is taking care of you. I have to admit I was afraid you'd let your independent streak keep you from agreeing to police protection. Even though you're obviously involved with Nash, it's a good sign that you accepted his professional help."

"What do you mean, good sign?"

"Maybe you'll break down and let him be the father and partner he wants to be."

Patience stared at her sister. Not from annoyance or humor, but flat-out shock.

Because she didn't know for sure what Nash wanted, but hearing the words *father* and *partner* fall out of Layla's mouth made her see the truth.

She wanted all of Nash. Friend, lover, father to her twins. Their twins. And she wanted it to be a permanent arrangement.

Had she waited too long to realize it?

The sun began to set after she arrived back at the clinic, washing the sky a pale peach and rose.

"Come on, Ruby." Patience led the stunning Irish setter, who'd had dental work done earlier, to the fenced-in area outside the clinic. She'd finally gathered the courage to walk out here on her own, the first time by herself since she'd witnessed the Lake Killer. In spite of her feelings of being watched, she felt safe at the clinic. And it wasn't night yet, so that helped.

Ruby walked carefully around the grounds, but got down to business in short order. Patience stood near her, looking out at the mountains beyond the lake. The water was as still as a mirror, reflecting the sky and stratus clouds.

A movement at the corner of her vision caught her attention and she instinctively tensed. And then laughed when she saw a herd of eight deer. They leaped over the fields just outside the woods that bordered the far left side of the clinic property. Something had spooked them. Probably a fox or coyote.

She eyed the fence that surrounded her and Ruby. Its purpose wasn't just to allow the recuperating dogs, when not on leash, to roam about without wandering off, but to keep predators out.

The deer darted back into the forest and she marveled at their speed and agility. Then froze. A tall man stood at the far edge of the woods. A man with silver hair stared at her. Even without binoculars, she had no doubt who he was.

"Ruby, come here." She tugged on the leash and got herself and the dog back into the clinic, locking the door behind her. One of the night-duty vet techs was down the corridor and she shouted for him to call 9-1-1, then get out of there. The Lake Killer didn't want anyone but her.

Patience hit the emergency siren button, located in the hall outside the kennels, and issued the command to hide in place and take cover. Then she handed Ruby over to another vet tech, instructing her to run, too.

Finally, Patience ran back to her office and got her weapon out of the safe. No way was the Lake Killer hurting her or her babies.

Nash strode through the K9 clinic, Greta at his heels. He'd made it there in record time after the emergency call came in. After checking in with the officers on scene, he'd convinced Finn that he and Greta were the ones to bring Patience out of the clinic. All the other K9 training center staffers were accounted for. As the evacuated team looked on, he'd donned body armor and suited up Greta, too. He was armed to the hilt. Nash's place was next to Patience, protecting her.

As was Greta's. The dog's gait resembled an eager trot as they approached Patience's office. Nash shoved aside the myriad emotions battling for position in his heart. Saving Patience required nothing less.

He knocked on her locked door. "Patience, it's Nash." He counted to two, prepared to break the door down. But she opened it first, and her face broke into a warm smile, just for him. Heat unfurled at the center of his rib cage and lit up his entire body.

Patience was a part of him. And she was alive.

"Hey yourself." Pulling her into his arms was as natural as breathing.

They embraced briefly, then he let Greta get some Patience love. She held the huge black, furred head in her hands and spoke sweet words to the canine. Her fingers gently explored where the cut had healed in record time.

"I hate that you saw that bastard again and I wasn't here." Nash's heart thumped in heavy agreement. He knew that Patience could take very good care of herself, no question. And she'd done the right thing, calling the RRPD.

"You're the reason I kept my cool enough to call it in and immediately come and get my weapon. It sounds like he's either been scared off or is waiting to break back in."

"We're not hanging around to find out. Let's get you out of here." Nash tapped his comms unit and spoke to

Juliette, who waited outside the clinic with the other officers. "I have Dr. Colton with me. Leaving now."

"Not so fast, Nash. Sit tight. Give us another minute."

Frustration pierced Nash. He knew he had to trust Juliette, for Patience's safety.

"Looks like we're holding in place."

"They've got it, Nash." She leaned against him. "How did your time with the Harringtons go? Let me guess—Hamlin's an arrogant ass and Devlin acted like he knows it all?" She was so good at distracting him, calming him down.

He laughed. "Pretty much, yes." He caressed her cheek with his thumb. "You know that Demi was really there, on his property. Technically, she broke into his house."

"If she did, it was for good reason. Trust me, now that I'm this far along with the twins, I understand what she's feeling, at least as far as being pregnant goes. No way would she risk her life or her baby's unless compelled to do so."

"I'm not arguing with you. Just saying that we need her statement at the RRPD."

"She doesn't trust anyone right now, Nash. I get that. To be honest, besides my sister, you're the only one I can fully trust. It's a tough place to be."

"You trust me?" He tried to go along with her attempt at conversation, but the whole time his mind was waiting for the signal to get her out of here.

"Of course I do. What I don't trust, who I don't trust, is the man I saw dumping that poor woman in the lake. Who I feel the RRPD may be apprehending as we speak. And I don't trust Hamlin Harrington marrying my sister. What kind of a man allows a woman to be bartered for his financial support to her father? A dowry is an archaic concept."

"It may be, but your sister is a grown woman. She has her choices to make, too."

"That's just it—she won't do anything to hurt Daddy." Patience sighed. "My sister and I are products of an absentee father. He was often physically there, for meals and such, but emotionally, mentally? All Fenwick Colton thinks about is how to keep himself at the top of the heap. Financial, political, community-wise, whatever. He may have been a kinder person when he was younger, when my mother was still alive. Who knows?"

"You think he married women so that they'd have a baby for him?" He saw that their dialogue relaxed her, so he continued to go along with it. What the hell was the rest of the RRPD doing? Where was the signal from Juliette?

"No. I think they figured out he wasn't all he'd sold himself to be. When they realized they couldn't fix him, they left."

"Yet you're in touch with your half siblings." The Coltons had a reputation as a tight-knit family. He'd never known the drama behind the billionaire clan.

"Yes, we all share a common bond, in that we survived having Fenwick Colton as a father. You saw him at the cabin, Nash. He's so self-centered."

"He might change when he meets his grandkids." Nash nodded at her belly. "How are you doing today?"

A smile wider than the lake spread across her face. "Wonderful. I felt them kick earlier. Lots of little flutters. At first I thought it was from drinking ginger ale—you know, the bubbles. But it was more definite. As soon as it happens again and you're with me, you'll have to feel for yourself."

His hands tightened into hard balls. The thought of feeling his children in her tight belly filled him with a sense of completeness he'd never known.

An explosion pierced the stillness and they both jumped. Patience screamed, "Nash!"

"Get down!" He watched as she grabbed her weapon and got under her desk. Hated that she'd already been through this, and had to again.

"Nash, we need you and Greta to clear the back hall-way." Chief Colton's command boomed over the audio system. "Leave Patience in her office."

Nash leaned across Greta and grasped Patience's face. He kissed her firmly, conveying his total confidence in her. "I won't be gone long—I won't even leave the clinic building. But I have to make sure no one out there needs help. I'll be on the line with dispatch."

"Okay." Their gazes held and the words that matched the emotions he'd been afraid to name were on the tip of his tongue. But not here, not in the midst of this kind of danger. He'd tell her he loved her on his terms, not some criminal's.

"Sit tight. I've got to take Greta, but we'll be right back."

"I know you will. And, Nash?"

"Yeah?"

"I—"

"Don't say it, Patience. Not yet." He stood up and left, before he couldn't.

"I'm approaching the back entrance." Nash spoke into his mic as he cleared the corridor, as ordered by the chief.

"Be careful, Nash. We still don't have him." Finn's voice sent fear rocketing through his system, but he relied on his training and years of experience to ignore it. Patience's and the babies' lives depended upon him.

"Copy." Greta stayed at his side, ready to attack as she kept stride with him.

They came up to the kennels.

"Clearing the kennels." He opened the door and motioned for Greta to go ahead of him, to use her nose to find any sign of the Lake Killer.

"Copy." Juliette's tense voice let Nash know they were still looking for the killer. They all were.

He moved to follow Greta into the kennel, but a blinding strike to his skull sent a shaft of pain through his body, just as he was pulled backward, the kennel door slamming shut with Greta inside.

Patience!

Before he had a chance to resist, darkness captured him.

Patience sat under the desk for what seemed like hours, but according to her watch was only eight minutes. She regretted not using the restroom before Nash left. The babies were continually pressing against her bladder and it'd been foolish to not empty it before going into full lockdown.

But the Lake Killer was out there. Staying safe took priority over bathroom needs.

There'd been no other sound from outside, nothing from dispatch over her phone or clinic intercom. She trusted Nash and the RRPD security patrol implicitly. But it didn't keep the cold snake of fear from coiling in her gut and making her want to scream. She gripped the weapon in her hand, missing Greta's protection.

The silence grew along with Patience's trepidation. No further explosions or gunshots sounded from outside. Even the patients in the kennel were ominously quiet. She tried to reassure herself that it was a good sign; if Gabby, the parrot, remained still and not a squawk left her formidable beak, then chances were no one was hiding there.

Patience forced herself to draw in deep breaths, hold the air and then release it forcefully in an effort to center herself. She couldn't ignore her bladder any longer. The bathroom was just off her office. She'd be in and out in a flash. Quickly and quietly she used the restroom, making it back into her office within two minutes. She huddled under her desk again, weapon ready.

Greta's sharp, protesting barks shattered the silence and sent chills of fear through her. The sound reverberated across the clinic as Patience held her weapon in front of her, ready to shoot.

Two gunshots in swift succession sounded a split second before glass rained down on her office's tile floor. She'd been here before, knew what it meant. The Lake Killer was back.

It was now or never. Patience eased from under the desk, keeping her body behind the furniture, but enabling a clear shot at the intruder.

She balanced her arms on the desktop and faced the man she prayed she'd never see again. Not free and threatening like this. She wanted him behind bars. Now she'd kill him before he hurt her or her babies.

The Lake Killer pushed her office door open and stepped inside, dragging a limp body behind him.

Nash. Her entire life, her future, her love. He'd killed Nash.

His cold killer eyes hadn't changed, except to have gained more evil in their depths. He held his pistol but, instead of pointing it at Patience, aimed it at Nash as he dumped him on the floor.

"Put down the gun or I'll kill both of you." His voice chilled her even more than his eyes.

Clarity kept her panic at bay. She had to keep the babies safe. "Drop *your* gun. You've already killed him." She gripped her pistol, waited for him to comply, while never expecting him to. She took aim.

"He's still alive." The killer kicked Nash, who let out a harsh grunt, even unconscious. "The dog's dead, along with all the animals in your kennel, unless you come out now."

Nash was alive! She didn't believe for one minute the killer wouldn't harm her, but she also knew Red Ridge police officers were just outside, and hearing everything over her phone. Somehow, they'd make it through this.

"Put your weapon down." She repeated her demand.

"We put them down together."

She'd never trust him. Where were Finn, Juliette, the rest of the RRPD? She didn't know how long she could keep the killer talking, or if she'd be able to distract him from what he want. Her. Dead.

Despair rose and she saw dark spots in front of her eyes. What was the point?

Nash groaned again, and the sound of his voice even in pain fortified Patience's resolve. There were two tiny beings inside her. She had to do whatever it took to save her babies. Which meant she had to save herself. If she shot the Lake Killer, he'd fire back. Even with a reflexive shot from him, chances were good she'd be hit, too.

"Now. Put your weapon down." She spoke slowly, constantly looking for a way to distract the killer.

"Drop yours or I'll crush his skull." The killer stepped on Nash's shoulder to prove his point, eliciting another long groan from him.

"Patience, you there?" Finn's voice came over the clinic intercom.

"I'm here. Suspect refuses to comply." The killer's eyes never left hers, and she sucked in a deep breath. She'd have to kill him. She briefly looked at her weapon, made certain her safety was off, but it was too much time. She looked back at the killer in time to see him lunge toward her with an object in his beefy hand. It wasn't a gun or a knife.

A syringe.

She screamed and aimed her weapon at him, but not before the sting of the needle pierced her neck. As her world spun and began to drift, she heard the Lake Killer's promise.

"I told you I'd be back for you, you bitch."

Chapter 20

Nash came to on the floor of Patience's office, his head throbbing, Greta's barking annoying as hell. His first thought was to get up and run, but to where? He heard Greta's barks, urging him to rise.

When he sat up the room spun, and he had to wait for it to stop. The Lake Killer… He'd knocked him out. Patience was gone, and the sight of her overturned desk chair and spots of blood on the floor terrified him. It also gave him the courage he needed to fight through the pain. Patience. He had to get to Patience. The bastard had her.

He moved as quickly as he could, which was too slow, too awkward. Leaning against the corridor wall, he caught his breath and remembered his comms unit, which he pressed with a trembling hand.

"Nash?" Finn's voice, if his battered brain was correct.

"Yeah. Hit. On head."

"Nash, stay there. We have eyes on the killer and we're moving in. Repeat, stay there."

Like hell. He pushed the kennel door open and Greta bounded out, but not to see if he was okay. She raced down the hall and disappeared.

She'd run out the back door. He leaned on the windowsill and saw her huge figure streak across the training field and through the open gate to the pier.

The lake.

Oh, God, no.

His plea wasn't answered as he looked to the water and saw a small motorboat moving away from the pier, toward the center of the lake. Steered by a man with silver hair, with the unmistakable shape of a woman slumped next to him.

Patience.

Nash immediately half hobbled, half walked to the exit. He'd never get to her in time, but Greta would.

"Nash, you still with us?"

"Where. Are. You?" He gasped with each step, his head screaming in pain. When he got to the door he walked out onto the deck and hung on to the railing, fighting for air. Struggling to keep Patience in focus. She was so still. A strangled sob squeezed out of his throat.

"Nash, listen. Stay put. The killer booby-trapped the clinic so that we can't move forward, not until we've cleared the area of explosives. You'll trip a detonation wire if you try to leave."

"I'm already outside." He kept going toward the pier, his breath returning. "She's in the lake with him. Greta's there."

"Copy that."

He ignored Finn and kept going. Nash got to the pier in time to see an image no man ever wanted to. As he watched, the Lake Killer dumped Patience's unconscious form over the side of his motorboat. It wasn't more than two hundred yards from the shore. Nash pulled out his weapon and took aim. He'd kill the bastard now.

Except Greta was swimming across the lake, and he saw her disappear under the surface. Fortunately, the Lake Killer wasn't interested in harming the dog, but only in escape, as he aimed his boat at the far shore and revved the engine.

Nash dropped his arm, knowing he'd never get a decent shot off now. He got himself into one of the RRPD launches, and as he started the engine, two officers and two EMTs jumped in next to him. The small motorboat rocked with their arrival, making Nash's stomach heave.

"We've got it, buddy." Juliette took over steering, and Finn shoved Nash onto the small bench as they raced across the lake toward where Patience had been dropped.

"Greta's doing her job, Nash. We'll get Patience out." Finn's voice was full of hope.

Nash clung to it. He had to believe she was still alive, that Greta would bring her up before it was too late. It was the single thread that held his sanity together.

They reached the site where she'd slipped beneath

the water just as Patience appeared to float to the surface. But it was Greta, nudging her up.

"Good dog, Greta."

"We've got her!" Juliette yelled, as she and Finn worked to bring her limp body aboard.

Nash's hopes were crushed when he saw the blue tinge to Patience's skin. It was the first Lake Killer victim all over again.

"No!" He pushed past them all, grabbed at Patience. Finn and Juliette pulled him back, giving the EMTs room to do their job.

"It's okay, Nash. Let them work." Juliette spoke as Finn held Nash's arms. "She'll be okay."

"How can you say that?" His entire life had died in this lake today and—

A loud cough was followed by sputters as Patience's lungs rejected the water she'd inhaled. Nash was afraid to look, but as the EMTs continued to work on her he saw her skin pinking up and hope crept back into his heart. When Patience asked for him with a raspy voice, Nash let the tears of gratitude fall.

They'd saved her.

Bright hospital lights and the smell of antiseptic greeted Patience as she woke up the next morning after a long night's sleep. The events of yesterday returned, and all she cared about was that the twins were safe, healthy. They'd survived the knockout drug the Lake Killer had stuck her with. As had she. She turned to find Nash at her side, watching her.

"How long have you been here?"

He gave her a slow smile as he stood and stretched, then came over to the bed and kissed her. "Awhile."

"More like all night?"

"Hmm." He kissed her again and she wished they were back at the cabin, alone, with the whole day in front of them to do nothing more than make love. She reached up to run her fingers through his hair and found a large bandage.

"Nash? What's this?"

He turned around long enough to let her see the large patch over the back of his shaved scalp. "I got a few stitches is all."

"And a concussion." She'd heard the EMTs talking on the ambulance ride to the hospital. Nash had ridden with her, and they'd checked him out.

"Minor. The outer swelling saved me from the worst."

"You saved me." She watched him as she spoke.

His face contorted into a grimace. "I wasn't there for you, Patience. Greta saved you."

She looked around the room. "Where is Greta, by the way?"

"She's at home. The kids miss her and she needed a day off."

"She saved my life." Tears welled and Patience knew she'd never be able to repay the dog.

"She saved us both." He kissed her forehead. "I'm going to go get some real coffee for us—there's a café downstairs. How does a caramel latte sound?"

"Like heaven."

"Be right back."

She watched him as he left, allowed herself the sight of his sexy backside. And realized she'd forgotten to ask if they'd caught the Lake Killer yet.

As she went to the bathroom, brushed her teeth and tried to make herself presentable, all she thought about was how incredible it would be if they were finally free of both the Lake and Groom Killers. She and Nash and the babies might have a chance at a real life, without the constant stress of being under attack.

As Patience walked back to her bed she heard the door swing open, and turned to give Nash a big smile.

And looked into the cold eyes of the Lake Killer.

Nash used his back to open the hinged door of the hospital room, holding two lattes and a bag of doughnuts. He froze when he saw the Lake Killer there, and Patience's wide eyes. To her credit, she didn't give away that she saw him enter.

"You'll never get away with this."

"I almost did yesterday, you bitch."

"There are more witnesses now, and you'll have to kill them all. It's not going to work."

"Watch me—ahhh!" Nash threw the treats to the ground as he jumped on the taller man's back and hauled him down. He vaguely heard Patience scream and call for help. The killer fought him, but Nash had the element of surprise and managed to subdue and hold him until security guards rushed into the room.

RRPD officers arrived ten minutes later and took the Lake Killer into custody. Finn was with them, and waited until the room cleared to speak to both Patience and Nash.

"You two have been through the wringer. I'm ordering you both to take a week off, no argument."

Nash shook his head, still a painful move. The adrenaline from capturing the Lake Killer must have dulled the pain temporarily. "I can't do that, Chief. The Groom Killer's still out there, and I've got my kids to take care of."

"It's paid leave, Nash. No arguments." Finn's eyes twinkled. "And I understand congratulations are in order."

Nash saw Patience smile, and more—he saw the relief in her features. The target on her back was gone, her stalker behind bars. "Thank you, Finn," she said warmly. "I agree with you—we need a break. But like Nash said, this probably isn't the time for it."

"No arguments from you, either, Dr. Colton." Finn nodded at them before he turned and left.

Nash looked at Patience, who sank onto the bed. "This has been too much for you."

She waved away his comment. "I'm good. You heard the doctors—the babies are, too. I can go home later today."

Nash knew this was the time to tell Patience where he wanted "home" to be. For both of them.

Patience saw the gleam in Nash's eyes after Finn left. It was the look he saved for her, the one that made her know he was thinking of nothing, no one else. Only her. Patting the space next to her on the hospital bed, she waited for him to sit, then took his hands in hers. His strong, sexy, dear hands.

"Nash, what I was trying to say before, in my office yesterday, is that I love you. And it's okay that you don't feel the same—this isn't my way of trying to get you to be more than you want to with the babies. But I had to tell you." A keen sense of happiness unfurled from her center, as if her heart was exploding in fireworks. It was absolutely the best thing she'd ever felt or done. She loved Nash.

He gave her his signature wide, sexy smile that made all they'd been through the past month melt away. "Babe, you're not getting off that easy."

"No?"

"I love you, too. And you're not going to raise these babies on your own."

Delight and pure love washed through her. "I'm not?"

"No. These babies will grow up with four older siblings, and with both of us." He touched her forehead with his. "Now's not the time, Patience, but when you're better, and my head's not so messed up, I'm going to ask you to marry me."

"You are?"

"Yes." He claimed her lips, this time in a promise to last the rest of their lives. "What do you think about that, Dr. Colton?"

"I think that when you do ask me, I'll say yes."

* * * * *

COMING SOON!

We really hope you enjoyed reading this book. If you're looking for more romance, be sure to head to the shops when new books are available on

Thursday
18th October

LET'S TALK
Romance

For exclusive extracts, competitions
and special offers, find us online:

f facebook.com/millsandboon

⊙ @millsandboonuk

🐦 @millsandboon

Or get in touch on 0844 844 1351*

For all the latest titles coming soon, visit
millsandboon.co.uk/nextmonth

Want even more
ROMANCE?

Join our bookclub today!

'Mills & Boon books, the perfect way to escape for an hour or so.'

Miss W. Dyer

'Excellent service, promptly delivered and very good subscription choices.'

Miss A. Pearson

'You get fantastic special offers and the chance to get books before they hit the shops'

Mrs V. Hall